Marteeka Karland

clubhouse gate six weeks
told Cain that Bones had
make a home." Who
motorcycle club?

"Beats the fuck o.... ..., ...
Torpedo clapped him on the shoulder. "Bohannon is sticking with the kids tonight. I'll see you at the Boneyard later tonight. Sword will be on you." Cain hated that the club put guards on him, but Torpedo wouldn't have it any other way. As vice president, it was his right to insist even if Cain disagreed.

"Fuck off." He flipped off the vice president as he turned away from him.

Cain looked around the sunroom where Miss Black had set up their school. From what Cain could tell, Suzie was kicking the boys' asses. Though he wouldn't put it past Cliff and Daniel to be doing subpar work intentionally in order to boost Suzie's self-confidence. He'd caught them doing little things like that for the girl. All three had been through a rough time in the foster system, and Bones had sworn to protect them from it ever again. The boys were fourteen and fifteen while Suzie was only eleven. The boys would have at least some say in their own situations while little Suzie would be at the mercy of the juvenile court system. They still hadn't gotten out of the kids how they'd heard about Bones or what exactly had happened to them, but the only time Suzie seemed normal was when Miss Black had her in class.

As if she knew they were talking about her, Angel turned her head, glancing at him over her shoulder. Fuck. He didn't need this. The second her gaze collided with his, she ducked her head and turned back again. Her shoulders hunched a little, and she studiously focused on the children.

"Fuck," he swore, this time out loud.

"Indeed," Torpedo muttered. "Go to the bar. Relax. Take one of the club girls and get laid, but let this go."

If only it were that simple. Maybe with enough whisky…

"Yeah. Boneyard, here I come."

The Boneyard was the bar the club owned and operated. In their little corner of the great state of Kentucky, the place was unique. Located in the boring little town of Somerset, it was the only biker bar in the area. While Louisville and Lexington both sported a few MC clubs, South Central Kentucky didn't have many other than local weekend warriors. The Boneyard, however, was always packed with one variety of biker or another. Didn't seem to matter if they were one-percenters or just bikers who wanted to get together to ride and support their community, anyone who was part of any MC club made it their business to be at the Boneyard when they were in the area. Probably because Bones kept it a safe place to do business. Neutral territory. All they asked was ten percent of the deal. They'd only had one club refuse to honor their deal. It hadn't worked out so well for the other club. Retaliation had been swift and brutal. None of it leading back to Bones, but the message had been received by everyone. The other ninety-nine percent of MCs just wanted the atmosphere. Cain suspected many legitimate clubs also sought one-percenter clubs to take care of business they didn't want to get their hands dirty with. As long as Bones made their ten percent, Cain didn't give a fuck what deals they struck.

Thirty minutes later, he had a shot of Jack Daniels down and one on the way. Another one waiting in front of him. He sat back in a corner, his back to the wall where he could see the entrance and the door leading to the back. The lighting was dim so he could disappear into the shadows easily enough and just watch the goings-on around him.

Cain prided himself in knowing every person who came into the Boneyard. When a new group entered, Data, their tech guy, used his techno magic to compile a full background on them before they left. By the end of the night, Bones knew everything about the newcomers and where their interests lay. While Boneyard was neutral territory, there were certain things Cain absolutely would not tolerate.

He was just starting to sip his third shot when little Miss Angel Black took a tentative step inside the bar.

Fuck.

She looked just as she always did. Sexy as fuck, dressed in a conservative, knee-length black skirt and a cream-colored blouse that came up to her neck with a black jacket. She had black hose and black kitten-heeled pumps with delicate straps that wrapped around her slender ankles. It made Cain wonder if she wore garters to hold up those stockings. Which made him hard as fuck.

She squinted, pushing up her glasses with one finger while scanning the interior, looking so out of place it was laughable. With careful steps, she approached the bar, looking warily around her. Pops was tending bar tonight. Maybe he'd warn her off gently, because she was about as out of place here as a nun would be. The older man and his wife were the moral compass of the club. Not official members, they still acted as mom and dad to all of them, especially their new charges. No one knew their real names or why they preferred it that way but no one pushed. No one judged.

"How are the kids doing?" Pops asked in greeting.

"Very well," she said with a smile. "I wanted to talk to someone about the education plan for them. Everyone says I need to talk to Mr. Cain. Is he here?"

"Just Cain, young lady." Pops smiled, setting a glass of ice water in front of her. "Unless you want the good stuff?"

She smiled, accepting the water and taking a sip. "No thanks. This is good."

Pops nodded in Cain's direction. "In the corner," he said, leaning closer to Angel. "Be careful with that one. He's a good man, but likes to be left alone."

"No worries there," she said, taking a gulp of water. "I just need to be clear about how to proceed with the children."

Pops smiled at her encouragingly. If Cain hadn't respected the old man so much, he'd have flipped him off. The last thing he needed right now was to have an intimate conversation with Little Miss Prim and Proper.

She turned in his direction. Cain's first instinct was to ignore her and leave. The less contact he had with her the better. That felt too much like running, though. Cain didn't run from fights. He didn't start them, usually, but he ended them. He could handle one small woman.

She squinted, and a sexy little crease between her perfect, dark brows appeared until she finally spotted him. Many women had approached Cain in this bar. Without fail, they gave him a sexy, sultry look and exaggerated the sway of their hips once they found him. Angel... didn't have to exaggerate. Anything.

There was a hesitant expression on her face, as if she wasn't sure if she really wanted to talk to him now she'd found him. Cain saw the exact moment her resolve kicked in. She took a deep breath, pushed those sexy glasses up on her nose again, and then made her way through the crowd to him.

Every step she took was like an awakening to Cain. A revelation. Like, before her, he'd never seen a woman. Never known what true sexuality and eroticism were. Her hips had a natural sway that seemed designed to drive him insane with lust. With every step, the blouse she had so tightly tucked into her skirt stretched over her torso, emphasizing those generous breasts. Without trying, she was everything that appealed to him on a physical level. Thank God she didn't clothe that unholy body of hers in leather. If she did, she could drive a pink Harley or some shit and he'd just lie down and take it. And a pink Harley was just sacrilegious.

"Mister, ah, I mean, Cain." She ducked her head nervously, tucking a strand of silky black hair that had escaped her prim bun behind her ear. "I wanted to talk to you about the children."

"Are they fuckin' up?" His question was gruff, meant to scare her away. Instead, she winced at his language, but said nothing.

"No. They're doing great. I just had… concerns."

"If they're doing great, I don't see the fuckin' problem." Cain tried to look annoyed, like she was wasting his time and he wasn't happy with her. In fact, he really hoped she'd stand up to him and insist on continuing the conversation.

"May I sit?"

Instead of answering, he just looked at her. Most men he knew cowered at that look. Not Angel.

Apparently, she took his silence as permission to sit where she wanted because she took the chair across the table from him.

"As you know, I'm straight out of college. I'm qualified to teach middle school and most basic high school classes. The problem I'm finding is, both Cliff and Daniel are way beyond the basics even though they pretend not to be. Suzie is even more advanced and tries so hard to do even better."

"The point, Miss Black?" he said impatiently. He needed her gone.

She took a breath before continuing. "My point is, these children need someone trained in teaching gifted students. All three of them could not only be at the top of their class, but could get any academic scholarship they want, with the proper instruction before they graduate."

"You sayin' you can't teach 'em? Why didn't you say that before we hired you?" Hard as it would be to find another teacher, this might be the answer to Cain's prayers. She'd leave, and he'd not have to worry about her anymore.

"I'm saying, I still have assessments to do yet, but while I can get them to graduation, they could all go much further than high school."

"Do you want the job or not, Miss Black? I'm tired of fuckin' around."

She pursed her lips. "Did you listen to a thing I said?"

Well, fuck. She had bite. "I heard every Goddamned word. I heard you. What I didn't hear is that you *can't* teach 'em. All I'm hearin' is there are others who could do the job better. That 'bout sum it up?"

She blinked several times. "I suppose that's exactly what I'm saying."

"Then either quit or get to work." He stood up from his chair and went to the bar, hoping like hell he was rude enough she'd just quit.

"Fine," she muttered. It wasn't what he wanted, but she left. Boy, did she leave. In her anger, that impossible ass swayed even more with her longer, quicker strides. He was so fucked.

Chapter Two

If she'd had another choice, Angel would have taken it. Private teacher for three children at a motorcycle club wasn't exactly what she'd had in mind when she graduated from college, but she had to pay the bills and her mountain of student loans. *And* she needed someplace safe to hide. Even though she hated giving up any security she might have found, she couldn't in good conscience put herself above the needs of the children she taught.

As she hurried out of the bar, she clenched her fists in frustration. Cain was less than helpful. She'd only been working with the children a week, but she had yet to figure out who exactly the children's parents were. All she knew was that Cain took responsibility for them. Any time she had questions, the club had referred her to Cain, who was more closed-mouthed than a clam. Then again, she kind of understood it. That was the way MCs seemed to work. At least, that had been her limited experience. Everything stayed close to the vest.

In the parking lot, motorcycles lined the gravel area, making her little lime-green Fiesta stick out like, well, like a hybrid car in an MC-bar parking lot. She took a deep breath before heading to her vehicle. She would do this, but, in her heart, she knew these kids deserved better. She also wasn't blind to the fact they'd been through hell. She didn't think it was from the people in this club. All three children seemed to practically cling to the members she'd met, always looking for reassurance. The only thing was, she needed to let Cain know her baggage. If he was responsible for these kids, he needed to know her sins.

And her connection to another MC, however brief. He'd likely send her packing and solve her problem.

"Hey there, little miss." A big, burly guy approached her, flanked by two equally big men. All three wore motorcycle jackets and jeans, their colors proudly on display for all to see. The guy who'd addressed her had on leather chaps over his jeans. All sported tattoos and beards, much the same as many other patched MC members she'd met. It wasn't their appearance that concerned her. It was their expressions. One stopped by a bike parked next to hers, grinning as if he'd just heard an amusing joke. His eyes glazed with a nearly maniacal lust. "Nice ride you got there."

"Uh, thanks," she muttered, unlocking the door with the fob just before she reached the car. Thankfully, she'd parked with the driver's door on the opposite side from the bikes. Maybe she could keep the car between them and her.

"Don't look much like you belong in a place like this, little miss," the same guy said. "Why not let us show you around?" The smile he gave her was more like a sneer. Yeah. She'd just bet they'd show her around.

"Thanks, but I was just leaving." She gave them a polite smile. Angel thought about telling them she'd had business with the Bones president, but just as quickly discarded it. One thing she'd learned during her brief stint in a club was that you kept business internal. Period. "Good day."

"Hold on!" One guy lunged for the door of her car, slamming it shut just as she'd opened it. "A club member offers to show you around, you don't turn up your prissy little nose at him."

"I wasn't turning up my nose at anyone," she said. "I was just leaving --"

The guy cut her off by grabbing her upper arms and shaking her slightly as he got right in her face. With his height, he had to bend down a little, but he also pulled her up on her toes with what seemed like little effort. "You're not hearing me, bitch," he said. His sneer was now an evil smirk. "We want you to come party with us. Now."

"I can't possibly --"

He cut her off with a hard slap to her face. Angel gasped in shock and pain. Her ears rang and her knees threatened to buckle. The biker had her firmly in his grasp again, peering down into her face. When she focused on him again, he gave her a satisfied look.

"Good. We know what you want. Girls like you come here all the time looking for a bad boy. Well, you found three. Now, we don't want no one thinking we took you against your will, so why don't you be a good little miss and tell us you'll go with us. 'K?"

Angel's heart pounded. She couldn't believe this was happening in a place like Somerset! Bad things occasionally happened, but never like this. At least, not that she knew of. She looked at him for a long moment, hoping she looked like she was trying to get her bearings instead of like she was weighing her options.

If she could get away, she could dart back inside the bar in hopes someone would help her. Then again, what if they all thought like these guys? The other club sure had. God! Why hadn't she learned her lesson the first time? She might end up worse off than she was now. No way was she setting herself up for rape -- or worse -- by these guys.

When the guy leaned in closer, probably to intimidate her, Angel snapped her head forward hard, catching his nose with her forehead. Blood sprayed everywhere.

The guy let Angel go to grab his nose, screaming, "Fucking bitch!"

The others grabbed for her, but Angel took off as fast as she could in her kitten heels on gravel and bolted for the door of the bar, yelling a strangled "Help!" As she should have predicted, she stumbled, turning her ankle and tumbling to the ground with a cry. One guy was on top of her a split second later. He brought his fist down, but only hit a glancing blow off her arm as she wrapped both arms around her head for protection. That did nothing to stop the kick to her back. She cried out again, rolling to protect her back by putting her front to the attack. At least that way, maybe they'd hit her legs and arms, where she'd tucked into a ball, instead of something vital on her torso.

As abruptly as the attack started, it ended. She heard a scuffle followed by swearing then a solid *thunk*.

"Whoa, man! Take it easy!"

"What the fuck?"

"You come to my bar and attack my people, you answer to me." The voice was gruff, angry-sounding. If she didn't know better, she'd say it was Cain's voice. She sincerely hoped that whoever it was had brought backup because three against one were bad odds.

Another *thunk* sounded, this time followed by a scream.

"All right, all right! We're going!"

"And don't come back. Tell Poacher the Scars and Bars are no longer welcomed at the Boneyard. He has a problem, you tell him to contact me."

"Come on, Cain! You can't ban us for a little fun! Bitch had it comin'! She'd been teasin' us all afternoon then refused to follow through!"

Another *thunk*. This time, instead of a yelp or a scream, a sickening gurgle, followed by a loud thud as someone hit the ground. Angel refused to peek under her arms to see in case the attack wasn't over.

"You just… Oh, man!"

"You can't do that, Cain! Poacher will declare war over this shit!"

"Again. He has a problem with this, you tell him to call me. Better yet, you tell him to come over and we'll… *chat*."

"You threatening our president?"

"I *never* threaten. Deliver my message and we'll see how this plays out."

"What you gonna do with Squat?"

Cain didn't answer. He moved between her and the two remaining bikers. Finally, Angel had the courage to peek through her arms, only to wish she hadn't. The man who'd attacked her lay on the gravel, a knife protruding from his neck. Blood was everywhere. No way could she stifle her whimper.

"You gonna leave or you want me and my brothers to cull the Scars and Bars even more?"

As if on cue, Angel heard several footsteps approaching them. They didn't sound hurried, just… *there*. As if the club knew their president didn't need the backup and were only there to watch the show. She scooted away carefully, keeping her back to her car. She hadn't made it much past the front bumper, anyway. If she were careful, she might get the door open and slip inside. Then she could mow down anyone she needed to to get the hell out of here. God!

She was so stupid! Running from one club straight into the arms of another.

"We don't want no more trouble," one of the two remaining Scars and Bars said, his hands up. "Consider us gone."

"I'll consider you gone when I no longer hear your rat bikes on my road."

The two looked like they wanted to kill Cain, but six more Bones members quelled them. Without another word, the two started up their rides and sped off, spinning gravel in all directions, including over her.

It was several seconds before Cain turned his attention back to her. It was all Angel could do not to sob. Now that there was no threat of kidnapping and rape, she just wanted to get in her car and get out of there.

She scrambled to her feet, reaching for the door handle, stumbling when her legs wouldn't hold her. Strong arms wrapped around her body, holding her upright. Instinct took over, and she fought like mad, snapping her head back only to land against a solid chest. She kicked and dug her nails into the arm around her middle but the man didn't let go.

"Stop!" The command growled beside her ear had the effect of rendering her helpless. There was just something about it that demanded full and immediate obedience.

Angel was so scared she could barely breathe. Her clothes were ripped and dusty with dirt and gravel, her stockings torn from her fall. Several scrapes stung her legs and arms. Her hair had come down and was now in a tangled mess. Not to mention she was bleeding from a cut at her temple. How it got there, she had no idea.

"No one will hurt you, Angel." That was definitely Cain. She knew not because she recognized his voice, but because of his reflection in the car window. His voice was different now than it had been any other time he'd spoken to her. It was gruff and raspy, almost a whisper brushed against her ear. "Let's get you inside and look at the damage."

"I just want to get out of here," she whimpered. God, she hated sounding so weak! Weak would get her nowhere. Not with these types of men. She knew that firsthand.

"How about I take you to the clubhouse and you can clean up?"

"Don't let the children see me," she begged. "I don't want to frighten them."

Her left side hurt like a bear where the guy had kicked her. When Cain scooped her up in his arms, she braced herself, unable to stop from stiffening with the sudden movement.

"Does it hurt?" Cain asked.

"I'm afraid I'm going to have a nasty bruise."

Cain didn't respond, just strode around the car, opened the passenger's side and placed her in. Next thing she knew, Cain was folding his large frame into her compact car. To say it was an ill fit was a vast understatement. He slid the seat all the way back and the steering wheel all the way forward and still looked cramped.

"Fuck," he muttered. "Either get a bigger fuckin' car or get a Goddamned bike." Then he started the Fiesta and pulled out of the parking lot, headed toward the clubhouse.

"I don't need a bigger car," she said. "And I can't drive a motorcycle."

He glanced at her but said nothing. The muscle in his jaw clenched and unclenched, betraying his irritation. Thankfully, the clubhouse was only a few miles down the road. The sprawling complex had looked out of place to her from the beginning. It wasn't anything like what Angel expected the first time she'd seen it. The place wasn't overly ostentatious or anything, but was like a compound, big enough for the entire club to actually live there. She had no idea if they did, but there had to be enough space for everyone she'd met from the club and more. Not only that, but the kids had their own rooms there, according to them.

Cain pulled her car around to the back and parked it. Without saying a word, he went around to her side and scooped her out of the car, carrying her inside.

Having finally caught her breath, Angel tried to relax and take stock of her injuries, but the adrenaline left her shaky and slightly sick. Not to mention that her she was aching more and more with every second. Angel raised a hand to her temple. Her fingers came back streaked with blood from the stinging cut.

"I cut my head," she said inanely.

"Uh huh," was his only reply.

He carried her with long, effortless strides to a large room smelling faintly of antiseptic and bleach. Setting her down on a padded table in the center of the room, he smoothed her hair back away from the cut, tenderly brushing his fingers over her skin. Then he seemed to catch himself and jerked his hand back as if she'd burned him, throwing her a scowl that made her want to crawl into a corner and hide.

"Is she all right? Pops told me what happened." The woman everyone called Mama hurried through the door to Angel's side.

"She's pretty banged up," Cain answered. "Maybe a concussion. Don't know. Not sure how she got the wound at her temple but it might be worse than it looks." He stood next to her, reaching for the buttons on her blouse.

Angel batted him away. "I'm fine." Looking at Mama she said, "If I could just wash away the blood and maybe put a Band-Aid on the cut, I'd be grateful."

"Nonsense," she said. "This is what I'm here for. I'll take a thorough look at your ribs and maybe get a CT of your head." Mama put on her glasses before gently brushing the hair away from Angel's temple to look at the cut. "Might need a couple stitches there. I'll know when I clean it up."

"CT scan? Don't you think that's overkill? Besides, I can't go to the hospital. I don't have health insurance."

Cain shrugged. "We have all the equipment we need here. If Mama thinks you need more, we'll take care of it."

"You what? No way you've got that kind of medical equipment. Besides the fact it would cost a fortune, aren't there all kinds of permits required because of the radiation?"

"Relax, sugar," Cain said easily, the endearment not making her relax at all. "We're more than just another MC. Mama has anything she wants. She wants diagnostic equipment? She has it."

Angel looked to the older woman. "But how do you know what it all means? I'm sure you can't just take a picture and it spits out a result. There has to be a doctor to read them."

She gave Angel a smile, one that said, *Honey, please.* "I'm a doctor, sweetheart. Retired. But I still remember a few things. And if I have a question, I know a few people I can trust to ask."

Did Angel have questions? Certainly! But she got the feeling she didn't really want to know anything more. This was a questionable group of people she didn't need to rile. That hard lesson had been learned and learned well. She looked at Cain. It was a mistake.

The man frightened her on a level she couldn't describe or understand. He was tattooed and scarred nearly everywhere she could see. His body was big and powerful, but the thing that frightened her the most was his eyes. They were dead. Like he could stick a knife in a man and twist it with one hand all while eating his breakfast with the other. His hair was a nut-brown and shaggy with strands of silver woven in, same as his beard. He looked like he hadn't had a real haircut in years. Like maybe he just lopped his hair off whenever it got in his way. His eyes were a piercing turquoise. The only exception to his lifeless gaze was when he looked at her. There was no denying Cain was hot as hell on the outside, but the looks he gave her told Angel he hated her. That negated any hotness in her book. There was this blazing intensity sometimes she couldn't ignore. It wasn't a good feeling. He focused on her so completely she was afraid the man saw through to her soul.

"You gettin' undressed or do I have to help you?" Cain wasn't smiling when he asked the question. Angel was pretty sure he was serious.

"I'll get undressed when you leave the room," she managed.

"Nothin' I've not seen before."

"Well, you haven't seen *me*," she said defiantly.

"Out, Cain," Mama said, a merry twinkle in her eyes. "I'll call you when you can come back."

"You check her out good," he demanded. "If there's a scratch anywhere on her body, I want to know about it, and you make sure it's treated."

Mama stopped what she was doing and turned her full attention to Cain. "Young man, I suggest you watch your tone with me. You're president of the club, but I'm still your elder."

Cain raised an eyebrow but said nothing, turning and leaving the room. Angel shivered. She'd bet no one ever talked to Cain like that. If she had to guess, Mama and Pops were probably the only ones who could get away with it, and she didn't think it was because of their age. There was a dynamic with the older couple she was missing but could feel in her bones. There was more here than met the eye. More to the whole Goddamned thing.

Chapter Three

Cain was angrier than he could ever remember. And not only because another club had assaulted someone at his bar. They would deal with the Scars and Bars, but he was more concerned at how he felt about the victim being Angel. He'd killed one man and would have killed two more if his brothers hadn't come outside to ground him. He would have killed the two and dumped them all on Poacher's doorstep, declaring all-out war. Not a wise decision on his part. He was still considering going after the other two men, killing them -- eventually -- and dumping them in the fucking lake a few counties upstream.

"Assuming you want the body disappeared?" Bohannon, the club's enforcer, was always near when there was trouble. Without asking, Cain knew the man had already cleaned the area of both the body and any blood spilt.

"I want them *all* disappeared, but the one will have to be enough."

"Consider it done. What about Scars and Bars?"

"Ban them. If Poacher shows up, only he is allowed in and he's to be escorted to me immediately."

"We'll keep an eye out for more of them. Don't figure they'll do what you tell them." Bohannon was as good a judge of character as anyone Cain had ever met. Just one reason he was the enforcer of Bones. Not that he had to be to predict the actions of the Scars and Bars. Any MC threatened in such an aggressive way would respond. They had to if they wanted respect. By that same token, Bones had to retaliate for them breaking rules on their turf. It was a vicious cycle.

"I want any threat dealt with permanently. No one fucks with us on our own ground."

Bohannon looked at him, a hard expression on his face. The man knew it had to be done but wanted to be sure he understood. There could be no mistakes with an order like this.

"Is she worth it, Cain? Because we both know this is about Angel. Not any disrespect Scars and Bars committed."

"The disrespect is enough to warrant action." It was a non-answer, and they both knew it. "Just see it done."

"You got it, brother."

This was bad. Never once had Cain let his personal feelings influence the business of the club, but Bohannon was right. This was more about Angel than he was ready to admit. Even to himself.

He watched Bohannon get on his bike and take off. There would be more bloodshed before this was over. While he trusted every patched member of his club to be thorough in the disposal, he hated putting Bohannon in this kind of position. The enforcer would do whatever Cain asked of him without hesitation, and Cain had just given him a task that would definitely get blood on his hands. He had to be careful. Though Cain didn't particularly care who he had to get rid of, Somerset was a small town. Nothing could lead back to the club or any of its members.

"Took me a while, but I finally got a better low-down on her." Data, the cyber guru of the group, had been working on digging up Angel's past since they'd hired her. Apparently, he'd finally struck gold.

"Give it to me."

"You're not going to like it." When Cain held his gaze without saying a word, Data raised his eyebrows but continued. "Girl was either a house mouse or a patch chaser. I can't decide which. Though several patched members brag about having her, no one can give me personal details. The only one coming close is a guy named Gremlin. Whatever she is, she wasn't anyone's old lady or even claimed by any one guy."

Cain recognized the name. "Which club?"

"Kiss of Death. Small club in Nashville."

"Gremlin's old man is the president. Slash."

Cain knew of the man. His club was one of the worst Cain had ever come across. The men in that club did everything from drug runs to human trafficking to just beating the shit out of any man, woman, or child they came across. Word had it they even had a pedophile ring. The worst of the worst. They were brutal to their women and kept a tight rein on their territory. Any children born into that group either toughened quickly or didn't last long. What in the world was a woman like Angel doing with that kind of MC?

"Fuck," he swore under his breath. "She a spy of some kind?"

"Can't say for sure, but my gut says no. Mostly because of the inquires I saw Slash had made once I started diggin'."

"Slash know who's doing the diggin'?"

"Cain," Data gave him a wide, superior grin. "Look who you're talking about."

"He say what he wants with her?"

"Only that she's property of the club he wants returned."

"Property of the *club*?" Cain had to think about that one.

"I know. Odd. The tone I got was more that she'd left without permission, but that could be a misdirection. Only thing I know for sure is that Slash wants her back and will come after her if he finds out where she is."

"You think she knows they're lookin' for her?" Cain had already dismissed the possibility she was a spy. Angel was many things, but she wouldn't make a good spy. Unless she was a much better actress than he thought. Cain was a good judge of character and, like Data, his gut said she wasn't an intentional threat. Which left another problem.

"I doubt it, but you know any club looking for an errant member won't let it go. Not a club like Kiss of Death." Data was following the same line of thought Cain was.

"So, the question becomes do we cut her loose or take her on?"

"A question for you and Torpedo to figure out." Data said, raising his hands in surrender. "Above my pay grade."

"Fuck," he said again, turning to go back into the clubhouse. As he expected, Torpedo was waiting in the great room where the club held parties and meetings with other clubs. The man always seemed to be able to read his mind.

"Something brewing?"

"We may have a problem."

"Has to be the woman."

Cain raised his eyebrow, not slowing his pace down the hall toward the infirmary. "What makes you say that?"

Torpedo snorted. "It's always the woman. We need Pops?"

"Yes."

Cain was aware of the other man taking out his phone but didn't wait. He made his way back to Angel and Mama. Best to get this over with quick.

* * *

Mama had put Angel through a battery of tests. Her touch was careful. Gentle. She'd been more than kind as she'd asked Angel exactly what had happened, keeping everything as clinical as possible. When Angel had let a few tears fall, the older woman had wiped them away gently and hugged her, assuring her she was safe now.

"I'm so stupid," Angel muttered as she pulled on the T-shirt Mama had given her to go with the gray sweatpants. Her clothes weren't a total loss, but they needed mending and she was grateful she didn't have to wear them home. Mama had also given her socks and canvas shoes. If only she'd had this outfit on instead of those stupid heeled sandals, she wouldn't be in this mess to begin with.

"Nonsense, child. You couldn't have known something like this would happen. Cain will make sure it will never happen again."

"I got that when he killed one of the guys who attacked me." Angel wasn't sure she'd ever get over that sight.

"Well, what did you expect? They disrespected a club in that club's own territory. They knew better and attacked you anyway."

"Mama," she said, looking her in the eyes. Angel knew she looked haunted. There was no way to hide that. Not from this woman. Mama and Pops both had a way of putting everyone at ease so they confessed their innermost secrets. "I'm in trouble. I knew better than to take up with another MC, but I did anyway."

Instantly, Mama's features hardened. "Explain, child."

Angel winced. This was the whole problem. If she told anyone in Bones why she was running, they could very well reach out to Slash or Gremlin. "I can't risk it, Mama. If Cain sees it as playing nice with another MC for favors, it's my life." She put her head in her hands. "I'm so screwed!"

"You're gonna to have to do better'n that." Cain. He stood just inside the doorway with Torpedo next to him. Pops moved in behind the two other men and crossed to Mama, putting his hand on her shoulder. Strangely, Angel got the feeling he was preventing Mama from doing something, not supporting her.

Angel looked up at Cain. She knew she was defeated. "Are you going to make me leave?"

"Depends on what you tell me." Cain's voice was soft. Matter of fact. "Best get it all out. You have one chance. I want the truth. All of it."

Angel wanted to cry but knew better. These people weren't her friends. They could give two shits what her problems were as long as it didn't affect the club. She was in big trouble. Out of the corner of her eye, she saw Mama pick up a syringe, but she made no move toward Angel. Pops tightened his grip on her shoulder. Angel met her gaze and knew Mama and Pops were as big a threat as any of the club members.

"I was finishing up my grad work at Belmont University when I met Gremlin. We went out a few times, but nothing too heavy. I was beginning to really like him. One night, at a bar near campus, I was with him. I'd had a little too much to drink, and he offered to take me home. I trusted him. He'd always been nice, if a little vulgar occasionally, but then, so was I. It was playful flirting. I thought. Only instead of taking me home, he took me to their clubhouse. Kiss of Death is the name of the club. I found out later Gremlin is the son of their president." She winced, turning her head a little. "That didn't keep him safe from Slash's wrath when he found me there, though." Slash had beaten the living daylights out of Gremlin.

"I take it Gremlin didn't have permission to bring in a new girl." Cain said.

"I have no idea. I was drunk when he brought me there. More so than I should have been. I'd only had a couple of drinks. No more than usual. During the night he kept giving me more and more to drink. I'm pretty sure more than one of them had sex with me over the course of the night, though I'm not sure how much was real and how much was my imagination. I was terrified! I don't want to know, either. I could barely turn over let alone fight them off. Besides, I was drunk out of my mind. I'm not even sure how he got me to drink as much as he did or if any of it was even real. He could have drugged me. I could have passed out and hallucinated. I just remember someone handing me a glass every now and then and telling me to drink. I was so thirsty and dizzy I couldn't think beyond the liquid in the glass." She shuddered, taking a breath, mortified but too scared to leave out anything. When Cain told her she had one shot at this, she believed him.

"Anyway, when I was finally able to get my wits about me, I'd been there something like three days. I figured that part out later. Slash had beaten the crap out of Gremlin and the rest of the club had been..." She couldn't say it. Taking a deep breath, she plowed on. "So I pretended to still be intoxicated and stumbled outside early one morning when everyone finally bedded down for the night. I pretended like I was going to be sick and then bolted. I wasn't with them long, but long enough to know I never wanted to see any of them again. I went to the first pharmacy I could find and got a Morning-After pill, then got the hell out of Nashville."

"Did you go to the cops?" Torpedo sounded as scary as Cain.

"No. I just wanted gone. Besides, I figured going to the police would only make them angrier. At least by just leaving I thought I had a chance of getting away from them."

"Say we believe you," Mama said, her fist still clenched around a syringe. Angel had no idea what was in the thing but she doubted it was a tetanus shot. "Why would you willingly head back into another club?"

"The children," Angel said quietly. "I just wanted a way to support myself until the end of the school year when teachers were being hired. Homeschooling three children seemed like the perfect option. Once I found out they were living with a club and had no discernable parents, I had to make sure they weren't being mistreated. I knew all three had been through something terrible from the first moment I met them, but after a few meetings with them, I knew it wasn't from this club. They look to all of you like you can walk on water and they expect nothing less, not like they fear you."

Mama visibly relaxed. Pops let his hand fall to his side and gave Angel a curt nod. Torpedo looked at Cain, who shrugged.

"The first thing she said when I told her I was taking her to the clubhouse was to not let the children see her so they wouldn't be scared. What do you think?" Cain was clearly asking Torpedo. As club president and vice president, they would assess the situation then bring it to the greater group. Angel knew her fate was being decided right before her eyes.

"I'll brief the others," Torpedo said. "We'll discuss it then decide if she's cut loose."

"What does that mean?" Panic seized Angel like a vice. "Cut loose as in you'll let me go? Or cut loose as in you'll turn me over to Kiss of Death?"

Cain looked at her then. His eyes were as chilling as ever, but something else glimmered in them she couldn't quite define. Something that scared her almost as much as the thought of being back in the hands of Kiss of Death.

"We'll let you know when we've put it to a vote."

Angel couldn't stifle the little sob that escaped her. "You can't turn me back over to them. They'll kill me."

"No, Angel," Cain said, taking a step toward her. "They won't. A woman like you they'd keep. Sounds like that's what they had planned from the beginning. Gremlin just didn't get the go-ahead on the plan or the woman from Slash. Once they had you, though, there was no way they'd have given you up."

"You think they're coming for me?"

"I know they are. They just haven't found you yet."

Angel knew she needed to get scarce. If she wanted to live, she needed to disappear and keep her head down. She knew she couldn't have lived with herself if she hadn't at least checked out the arrangement with Cliff, Daniel, and Suzie. Those kids had been through at least as much as she had. Probably more. She'd done the right thing but it might be her undoing.

Cain turned to Mama. "Don't let her leave until we straighten this out."

"Cain," Pops said. "She's got a good heart."

"That might be, but she's in the wrong place. I have to put the good of the club ahead of any outsiders. If Kiss of Death is a danger to us, we may not have any choice but to turn her over, or at least put them on her trail."

"You believe she's telling the truth?" Angel wasn't surprised the question came from Mama. The woman wasn't what she'd seemed at first. Which was just one more thing that frightened her about this situation.

"On the surface, yes." Cain's gaze never wavered from Angel's. "She's confirmed everything we dug up on her. The circumstances will need to be looked at, but I think that will be easily accomplished. Once we do, we'll decide what to do with her."

That was all she could take. Angel broke down into sobs. She was on the floor a moment later at Cain's feet. "Oh, God! Please!" Her behavior was mortifying but she couldn't seem to stop herself. "I can't go back to them. Please don't send me back! I'll disappear! I'll never mention you or the club or the children to anyone. I'll just be gone. No one will ever know I was here." She clung to Cain's pants leg, tears streaming down her face. "I can't do what they'd make me do! I just can't!"

"That's enough," Pops murmured gently, pulling Angel to her feet, wrapping an arm around her. Mama patted Angel's shoulder. "Do what you need to do, Cain, but work this out."

"Fuck, Pops! Just... *fuck!*"

"You're an intelligent man. *Work it out.*"

Angel found Cain's eyes, looking at him, wanting to look into them before he left to decide her fate. There was a hardened resolve there, one she couldn't decipher. He'd already made up his mind. For good or ill, this man knew her fate.

Chapter Four

Cain stalked into the meeting room. As far as he was concerned, this was a mere formality. He needed the approval of the club for this, but approval or not, Angel was staying. Hell, who was he kidding? Angel was his. He wasn't making her leave, and he damned sure wasn't turning her over to Kiss of Death. He would protect her with all the weight his colors afforded him. If that meant dragging Bones into a war with another club, he couldn't think of a more worthy reason. Anyone who went against him could get the fuck out.

"We're not cutting her loose, are we?" Torpedo had run with Cain since their days in the Navy. If anyone knew him, Torpedo did.

"No," Cain said. "I don't know if I can make a convincing argument for the others."

"You making her yours?"

"I am." There was no hesitation when Cain spoke. Just saying it hardened his resolve. "She's mine."

"Not sure she'll go for it."

"She doesn't have a choice."

"Cain, you can't use this as a condition of her safety. She'll hate you forever."

"Then I'll just have to make her want to be with me, won't I?"

Torpedo snorted then clapped him on the shoulder. "That you will, brother."

Torpedo had put out the word. Club members filed into the meeting room one or two at a time for the next thirty minutes. Not surprisingly, every single one of them was close. No doubt they'd heard about the problem with Scars and Bars and were closing ranks.

All the patched members sat around talking. Any prospects present waited instructions. Cain looked at each of them -- member or prospective member alike -- as he sat down at the big table where the club conducted business. All of them were good men. Several of them had been in the service with him. Those who hadn't, worked assignments with him through the contracting company he now owned. All of them had killed, but never indiscriminately. There was always a justifiable reason, and that reason researched thoroughly unless someone was in immediate danger. Since their solutions to those types of problems tended to be permanent, they had to be sure of what they were doing.

"I'll cut straight to the point," Cain said. "Angel Black is on the run from a club in Nashville called Kiss of Death." There was silence, everyone giving Cain their full attention. "During his search, Data discovered Slash, the president of Kiss of Death, wants her back, that she's property of the club and didn't have permission to leave. She says Gremlin, son of the president, took her against her will."

"Any truth to her story? I mean, was she taken against her will?"

Cain looked to Data, giving him every opportunity to tell them Angel was lying.

"I'm pretty close to confirming her story. A few members I talked to tried to make her out to be a patch chaser, but she was only there a few days and was drugged the entire time."

"You're sure?" Cain said, pinning Data with his gaze. "You found all that online?"

"Dark web chats. They think they're safe so they talk more freely than they would otherwise." He tossed several pages of printed chats in the middle of the table. "It's all there. Everything I found. Short of it is, that girl went through three days of hell. She told the truth about that, so I'm inclined to believe her when she says she's here because she wanted to make sure the children were in a safe place."

"Wait. What?" Bohannon held up his hand. "She thought we were harming the kids?"

"She didn't know," Cain qualified. "Apparently, she was looking for work until schools were hiring teachers. She came across us, found out the kids were in the care of an MC and took it upon herself to make sure they weren't being harmed. Likely, she thought it suspicious they were being homeschooled instead of going through the system."

"Fuck." Bohannon was nearly as upset as Cain. The men met gazes and Bohannon relaxed. "I'll risk war with anyone who'd kidnap and drug a woman to hold her prisoner."

"Are we even sure if they know where she is?" Goose, one of the Army Green Berets in the group, asked.

"Not likely," Data said. "Yet. From what I can tell she's been careful, but she didn't stay off the grid completely. She's used her debit card a few times. Since she's been working for us, she's been able to use cash, but if they've got anyone even decent at working computers, they'll find her."

"Is there a point to this meeting other than information sharing?" Bohannon wasn't vice president, but he was usually the one who called Cain out when he knew Cain had already made a decision before a meeting. He didn't do it with malicious intent, only to keep Cain honest.

"Bastard," he muttered. "This is why no one calls you Bohannon, like you preferred. In that TV show,

Bohannon was as much of an asshole as you are. I could easily see you killing a man in a fucking confessional booth same as he did. You're just as cold-hearted as he was."

"Noted," Bohannon said, crossing his arms and sitting back. "She your woman?"

That got everyone looking at Cain with raised eyebrows. The club had been together for nearly fifteen years. In all that time, Cain had never had a woman for more than a night or two. Even the patch chasers in their club rarely had him more than once or twice. He'd never even come close to claiming a woman.

Cain thought about telling them the strict truth. She wasn't but she would be. Instead, he took a more direct approach. It was more for Angel and they'd all know it. They'd been together too damned long not to see through each other.

"Yes. So keep that in mind when she's wearing those tight little skirts she thinks are so prim and proper."

Chuckles all around.

"So," he continued. "Be mindful there's another club out there looking for her. She's not fully one of us yet, but she will be. We protect our club."

"To the death!" they all said. It was their mantra, of sorts. Most of them had fought together in wars or something resembling war. The rest had been on the recon side of things. Either way, they were all used to having each other's backs. To the death was literal for them. They would protect every man, woman, and child under the protection of their club with their last breaths.

"Keep your eyes and ears open. Anyone hears anything about Kiss of Death or Slash or Gremlin, you make it known."

"What about Angel?" a Marine sniper they'd dubbed Dead Eye asked, a knowing smirk on his face.

"What about her, and I caution you to be careful here." Cain narrowed his eyes, giving the other man a killing glare. The look didn't faze Dead Eye in the least.

"Well, I only wondered if she knew she was under our protection."

"Why would you ask that?"

"Because I'm pretty sure, unless one of the prospects has changed rides, that little lime-green Fiesta of hers just booked it out of the parking lot."

"Fuck!" Cain ran to the window just in time to see Angel's car skidding onto the road as it spun out and fishtailed onto the asphalt. "Little hellion! I told Mama and Pops to keep her in the infirmary!"

He rushed out of the meeting room to find Pops shaking his head, his arms crossed over his chest. "You need to teach that one some manners, Cain." The older man wasn't angry. In fact, unless Cain missed his guess, he'd been snickering just before Cain approached.

"What'd she do?"

"Pretended to need to go to the bathroom, then bolted. Mama's furious. Wants to tranq her ass until you can explain things to her."

"Sounds like a pretty sound idea." Cain muttered.

"Cain," Pops started, a worried look on his face. "She's spooked. I don't know what you boys decided, and I don't want to know. But I know in my bones she's a good girl."

"She's mine, Pops. I won't let anything happen to her."

The old man looked startled, then grinned. "Well, then. Good." He clapped Cain on the back. "Go collect her. She know?"

"She will."

* * *

Angel could only remember being so terrified one time in her life. The day she fled Gremlin. Now, she was running from a group who would likely turn her back over to the very men who had drugged and probably raped her. How could anyone do such a thing? She'd never thought it was the MC culture, though she figured some clubs followed their own rules and no one else's. She'd heard that ninety-nine percent of clubs were law-abiding citizens, most of them banding together even to do community service in one form or another. What were the odds of her stumbling on two one-percenters back to back? Her judgment seriously sucked.

Her car sputtered. She mashed the gas. It sputtered again and the engine cut out. Apparently, her car sucked as badly as her judgment. She hadn't even made it a mile down the road. She pulled to the side of the road and cranked the engine. It turned over, but didn't fire. Glancing at the gas gauge, she saw why.

Empty. She could have sworn she had at least a half a tank!

She opened the door, not really sure why she was getting out other than it just seemed like the thing to do. The second she did, she heard the rumble of motorcycles coming after her. Immediately, she ducked back inside and closed and locked the doors, frantically considering hiding in the back seat under her emergency quilt left over from the winter.

No. She might be scared out of her mind, but she was no coward. She'd face these guys with her head high.

With an angry huff, she opened the door again and slammed it shut just as the first bike pulled alongside her. Of course it was Cain, with another man she didn't know on the back. Cain didn't get off the bike or even shut it down. He just handed her a helmet without a word. The other man got off the second the bike stopped and stalked toward her, gas can in hand.

"I'm not --"

"You are. Now, Angel." Cain was implacable. This wasn't a man one argued with.

"You siphoned my gas, didn't you? You can't keep me here."

"On the fuckin' bike. We'll talk back at the clubhouse."

The other guy moved easily behind her and started to refill the gas tank.

"Angel," Cain said, turning her attention back to him. "On the bike."

It was against her better judgment, but, really, what else was she going to do? They were in the middle of nowhere, several miles from the city. Rural didn't even begin to describe the area of the two-lane road surrounded by forest. If they wanted to kill her instead of taking the trouble to hand her over to Kiss of Death, they were in a fantastic place for it. At least this way, maybe she could talk them out of harming her.

"What about my car?"

"Taken care of. Now quit stallin'."

Still reluctant to get on that thing with him, Angel took her time putting on the helmet until Cain simply snagged her wrist and tugged her toward him. Once she'd settled on the running machine, Cain reached behind him and pulled her snug against his body. She bunched his jacket in her hands, refusing to put her arms around him. It just seemed too intimate.

"I suggest you hang on," he commented with a smirk.

"Just go," she snapped. He did. With a girly squeal, Angel lurched backward as the bike took off, her arms tightening securely around Cain's waist. She could feel him chuckle, deep inside his body where she was pressed so tightly. Fucker. He'd probably taken off so abruptly on purpose.

Angel expected Cain would take her back to the clubhouse. Instead, he passed the structure and sped on down the road, deeper into the woods. She knew the road well. She'd driven it many times down to the dock to feed the ducks. There were a few houses along the bank she'd admired. They weren't fancy or anything. Lake houses, she termed them. Most were used only during the summer months by what locals dubbed the Indiana and Ohio Navy. The lake was a source of tourism and recreation as well as a source of fresh water for the whole region across several counties.

Cain pulled into a garage attached to one such house. This one seemed to have a great view of the lake. He led her inside and Angel let him, not saying a word as he opened the door for her. Inside, the house was wide open. The kitchen and living areas were one big room. Split stairs went to the second floor landing where, presumably, the bedrooms were. There was nothing fancy about the place. The carpet was a flat, rugged variety, designed to clean easily and not hold dirt or mud. The very spacious kitchen was spotless without a crumb anywhere. Only the coffee pot had a small amount of dark liquid still in the bottom.

"What's this?" she finally asked. "Nice house." Cain just looked at her as he leaned against the bar, one hand resting on his hip. When he didn't answer, Angel crossed her arms over her chest and stared right back at him.

"This is my home," he finally said. "It's where you'll hide out for a while."

"Hide out? Is that code for you're keeping me prisoner?"

"Not at all." He straightened slowly, a ripple of grace and muscle. Cain reminded her of a big ol' cat. One stalking a mouse. "We checked your story. As far as we can tell, you were completely truthful. What you don't know is that it's Slash who's hunting you. Not the rest of the club."

Her stomach rolled and she was afraid she'd be sick. "Slash?" she whispered. "Why? He was the one who beat Gremlin to a bloody pulp for bringing me there in the first place."

"Combination of things, I imagine. You're a beautiful woman for one. Likely, the beatin' to Gremlin was as much to assert dominance over his son in order to take the woman he wanted. Also, I imagine he didn't like you just leavin' without permission."

"What are you going to do with me?"

"Fix you a cup of coffee," he said, meandering around the bar to the counter and washing out the container before starting a fresh pot. A few minutes later, he handed her a steaming mug, scooting cream and sugar her way.

"You'll understand if I don't accept drinks from others." He raised his eyebrow but said nothing, only took a swig of the liquid before handing it back to her.

Reluctantly, she took it. Mostly because it smelled good and, really, what could it have in it if he drank it himself?

"Your room is up the stairs on the left. Bathrooms are there," he pointed to a closed door next to the stairs, "And directly above that on the second floor. Deck out back wraps around the house. If you want to go for a ride on the lake, just say the word. I have a private dock below us."

"You're staying with me." It wasn't a question.

"Until this is worked out, yes. You're under the club's protection, but under mine specifically. It means everyone associated with the club -- patched members and prospects -- will protect you as if they were protecting me."

"Why would you do that?"

He just looked at her. Then went back around the bar to climb the stairs. Angel followed, unsure of what else to do and needing more answers. "Don't try to leave without me. Club members are posted in the woods watching the house. They'll know, and they'll stop you. I won't be happy."

"Where are you going?"

"To get some sleep. I was up all night. I suggest you get rest as well. Got a feeling you won't get much over the next few days."

"What does that mean?"

He didn't answer. He also didn't shut the door to his room.

Chapter Five

Angel sighed and turned slowly to wander across the landing to the other bedroom. She was so confused! She should be running instead of camping out with the scariest, sexiest man she'd ever met. As she quietly sat on the bed, she realized she could see straight across her room into Cain's. He stretched before whipping off his shirt. Tattoos decorated his body along with a few scars. She had a feeling he had more than a few but she couldn't see from this distance.

Before her fascinated gaze, Cain rid himself of his clothing. All of it. Ignoring her, he moved around the small but spacious room. She heard the window being lifted. Then she watched him fold his clothing neatly before laying them in a nearby chair. Several times, he stretched or rubbed a muscle in his thigh or arm. Angel wanted to go to him. See what the problem was and if she could help him work it out. His lithe movements completely mesmerized her.

Oh, who was she kidding! She just wanted an excuse to run her hands over his magnificent body. Muscles bunched and ridged the entire length of him. Washboard abs, a stunningly thick chest, brawny arms, and thick legs -- he was like an exquisite sculpture. Why that was foremost on her mind instead of escape, she had no idea. The last time she'd been in this particular situation it hadn't worked out so well for her. Of course, she'd been drunk, probably drugged, and restrained most of the time. This time, however, she didn't think they'd hurt her. If they'd planned on harming her, they'd have already done it. And they'd have done it humanely. With a quick slash to the throat or a clean break of her neck. They were killers, no doubt. But they didn't needlessly torture their prey.

Cain continued to ready himself for bed, moving around the room, gloriously naked. The hollows in the sides of his ass seemed to taunt her. As did that glorious Adonis belt. Helpless to look away, Angel watched until he sat on the edge of the bed. Through the whole thing, he ignored her, never so much as glancing her way. Every time he turned, her breath caught. He was a very large man. In all respects. And, good Lord above, he was... *aroused*! How she wanted to get on her knees in front of him for a better look! She wanted to explore every glorious inch of his body. And his cock. She'd run her hands up those strong thighs around to his rock-hard ass and cling as she took that long, thick cock deep...

What the hell was wrong with her? Angel stiffened and deliberately turned her back to him. She had to get herself under control, because her raging thoughts would only end in heartache at best. If he turned out to be as psycho as Gremlin, she could end up dead.

"You know, you could always sleep in here with me." Cain's voice made her shiver with need. The wicked, sinful call had her turning to take a couple steps toward him before she stopped herself. His warm chuckle told her he'd noticed.

"I'm good," she managed to squeak out.

"If you change your mind, I'm right here," he said. Angel couldn't help but glance his way. He lounged on the bed, propped on one elbow. His cock stood out proud and ready. As she watched, he dropped his free hand to it and gave a lazy stroke.

Angel couldn't stifle her groan. That man was sin. Lying there with that irresistible smirk on his face, lazily pleasuring himself, he looked like Satan himself, tempting her to the dark side. She marched to the door and would have shut it.

"Stop," he commanded, his tone now deadly and serious. "Doors open."

"Why? There's no need --"

"If there is a problem, I need to know. Also..." He grinned at her, taking another lazy stroke. His smile in no way reached his eyes. "I want to know if you try to escape."

"So, you *are* holding me prisoner."

"Not at all. I'm keeping you safe." He lay back, stretching out on the big bed, his hand still around his cock, but no longer pumping. One brawny arm was folded behind his head, one knee bent so she got a grand view of those heavy balls and that cock that was pointed due north. He didn't try to look at her, just lay back relaxing. "I'd prefer you to be in here with me, though, not necessarily for the sole reason of keeping you safe."

If there was such a thing as instant meltdown, Angel was experiencing it now. The naughty images he invoked with that seductive tone of voice were nearly her undoing. She sat heavily on the bed, unable to look away from Cain's supine form. The chuckle he emitted at her reaction infuriated her, but there was nothing she could do about it. Her body was weak.

"Bastard," she muttered.

"Unquestionably."

"Why? I'm nothing to you."

There was a silence in which Angel didn't dare breathe. Having asked the question, she wasn't entirely sure she wanted the answer.

"Angel face," he said softly, compelling her to look at him without actually ordering her to. When she did, the intensity she saw made her wish she hadn't. "I'm being nice to you. Going slow and not taking something you're not ready to give yet. I've claimed you in front of my club. That part's done." Dizziness swamped Angel at his words. And an unwelcome desire she knew better than to act on. "The only thing I'm waiting for is you. Once you're ready, I'll make you mine. My old lady. Once you wear my property patch, no MC will even look at you without risking my wrath and the wrath of my brothers."

"And you'd do this just to keep me safe?"

"Not *just*." He sat up then, a swift move that took her breath. He stood and stalked toward her. Muscles danced with every movement of his body. Powerful shoulders, sculpted arms and chest, rippling abs, thighs bunching with each step. It was more a stalking than anything as casual as walking toward her. She'd thought of him like a big cat before. This proved it. Self-preservation kicked in and she stood, ready to bolt if need be, and knowing it would be futile. "You need to understand something you're not exactly ready for, given what you've been through recently. So, I'll just say it's in my best interest to keep you safe. I can tell you that I'll also do everything in my power to keep you happy, so don't worry about anyone mistreating you."

"You going to tell me what I'm not ready to know? Because just as you gave me the ultimatum that I had one chance to tell my story, I'm giving you this one chance to be honest with me about what you want from me."

"Be careful, Angel face. I know you're not ready, but I'll definitely tell you."

He took another lazy step toward her, his cock bobbing with the movement. Angel stared in fascination as it grew and pulsed before her eyes. Why was he aroused? Probably because she was a woman in his domain and at his mercy.

She couldn't help moistening her lips as she gazed at him. "I just need to know," she said absently. "To know what I'm up against and what to expect."

Suddenly he was standing close enough for her to reach out and brush his cock with her fingers. She longed to do just that. Could nearly feel the steely length of him hot in against her fingers.

"Why do I want to keep you safe?" His voice was a gravelly whisper, further exciting her. "Because, Angel face, you're worth it. Precious beyond compare. I have no intention of letting you go once this is done. You'll be mine for as long as I decide. After that, you can go wherever you want. Until then, you'll be part of Bones. As my old lady."

She gasped, knowing she was reading way more into this. "You said that before. Doesn't mean any more now than it did a minute ago. You'll pretend I'm your old lady, then let me go when the danger has passed. You're not telling me anything."

"You're trying to make it into what you want to hear," he said, an amused grin tugging at his lips. "I'm being literal. You're mine, Angel." He cocked his head, shaking it once. "Maybe I wasn't being entirely honest. Even with myself. I said once I was done I'd let you go." He shook his head slowly. "I'll never be done with you. The reality is, once I fuck you, I'm keeping you."

That was it. Angel's legs gave out, but Cain was right there, wrapping his arms around her before she could collapse to the floor. There was a brief thought she should struggle, but once Cain had her, his arms holding her tightly, his body surrounding her with a delicious, male heat, Angel knew she was lost.

Her hands landed on his bare chest, her fingers curling into the muscles. She sighed, tilted her head up, and looked into his amazing sea-blue eyes. There was no stopping this. Amazingly, it wasn't Cain who made the first move. With a soft cry, Angel lunged for him, mashing her lips against his before she realized she'd done it. His delicious, exotic scent enveloped her like a warm blanket, a mixture of motorcycle fumes, clean sweat, and musky evergreen. His arms were so strong, wrapped around her like twin bands. Like he never wanted to let her go.

He met her kiss with a heated one of his own, his masculine groan fueling her own needy whimper. Fingers threaded through her hair, bunching there and forcing her head back to better accept his kiss. Just like that, Cain took over, sweeping his tongue inside her mouth like a conquering hero.

Had Cain not already been holding her securely to him, Angel was sure she'd have fallen to the floor. Since she'd already sagged against him, Cain took her weight with little effort. She wasn't altogether sure her feet were even still on the floor. Knew they weren't when he walked them to the bed.

Cain sat her on her feet before whipping her shirt over her head. Instead of his hands going to her breasts, he pulled her roughly against him once more, fusing his mouth to hers again while his big palms spanned her back. Wicked flicks of his tongue made her dizzy with lust. His hard chest, roughened with a light dusting of hair, tickled where her bra didn't cover her skin, adding to the sensations already spiraling out of control.

His cock pressed insistently against her belly, throbbing as if begging for attention. Somewhere in the back of her mind, Angel knew this was exactly the wrong thing to do. Cain had baited a trap, and she'd sprung it, now caught in his sensual web. It did little good to remind herself of all she'd been through at the hands of the other MC. She knew in her bones that this club was different. These people were different.

Bones. Ironic.

The next thing she knew, he'd pulled her bra off over her head, stretching the thing so she thought it would snap. Once again, instead of pawing her or dipping his head to suck her, he mashed her against him, this time with a deep, satisfied groan. His big body shuddered around her, as if the mere sensation of her bare skin flush with his was nearly an orgasmic high.

"Like the way you smell," he said, his nose in her hair right at her ear. "Sun and sex." Then he took her mouth again. Angel might have started this little interlude, but Cain would obviously control the path it took.

He trailed his lips down her neck, his hands sliding around her sides to mold her curves as he knelt before her. The wet heat of his tongue left a cool trail in its wake. He moved from the valley between her breasts to the underside of one, to her ribs and down her side. When he knelt in front of her, he tugged her sweat pants down until they pooled at her feet. Along with her panties.

Angel whimpered, reaching for his shoulders to steady herself. How her rubbery legs were holding her up, she had no idea. Each touch of his lips on her hip, her belly, her lower abdomen, made her tremble all the more. Her nipples ached and her pussy throbbed with need. Moisture leaked from her. She could feel it sliding down the inside of one thigh. The more he touched her, the worse the need. Effortless on his part.

And just like that, Angel knew she was way in over her head.

Just when she was about to thread her fingers through his hair and guide him to her aching sex, Cain stood and scooped her up into his arms. She thought he'd toss her to the bed. Instead, he turned, carried her to the door, and kicked the door shut. Then he carried her to the bed and laid her down as gently as he might a sleeping child. He blanketed her body with his own in short order, wedging his hips between her thighs.

Arm clamped around her back, Cain rolled them slightly, reaching for the bedside table and a box of condoms in the drawer. They never broke contact as he did. He rolled back with the box and broke the seal with a jerk of his finger. He pulled out a packet, ripped it open with his teeth and rolled it down his cock one-handed as he once again found her lips with his. Angel's heart pounded madly. Somewhere in the back of her mind, she knew this was a bad idea, but her body was having none of that. She knew it wasn't smart, but she *needed* him to take her. To fuck her with passion and desperation. Because she didn't want to be the only one feeling so out of control.

Finally, he wrapped his other arm around her, lifted his head, and surged into her, all the while looking into her eyes as intently as the big cat she'd equated him with. The pain was instant but fleeting. Full and burning. She wasn't a virgin, but he was large. Thick. It was more discomfort than actual pain, but almost enough to clear her lust-fogged brain.

Once seated all the way inside her, Cain didn't move. Just held himself there while she cried out and arched her back, wanting more but needing to adjust to his size and length. It took several seconds to realize he wouldn't give her what she needed right away, and she took calming breaths, squeezing her eyes closed, trying to get herself back under control. When she opened her eyes and looked into his, she knew it was yet another mistake on a huge list of them.

"That's right," he whispered, the sound somehow like that of one sentencing someone to a particularly unpleasant punishment. "You know you belong to me now. Don't you." It wasn't a question. Angel couldn't say anything. She was in a twilight between fear and desire, a haze that wouldn't completely lift to let her reason at a higher level. When she opened her mouth to answer in the affirmative before even questioning herself, her breath hitched. How could he make her so mindless she couldn't argue with him? Something she'd uttered in the heat of the moment she might be able to retract, her indiscretion not something he'd hold her to, but she doubted it. She pressed her lips together tightly.

"Oh, no," he said, rolling his hips in a lazy move, quite the opposite of his desperation earlier. "You don't get to think about it. Don't think. *Feel!*" He found her neck with his mouth again, first licking and running his lips back and forth, then biting down sharply. "*Answer me*," he hissed.

"Yes," she gasped, the sound nearly a sob of desperation.

In praise, he withdrew from her before sliding back inside in a measured movement. "Listen to me, because I'm only saying this once." He continued to slide in and out slowly. Her body relaxed with every thrust, letting him glide through her folds more easily with each forward progression. "*Mine* means no one else gets to touch you. Not someone you meet at the bar to dance, not any lover you've had past or present. No one but me. From this point forward, you're with me. I say when you leave. Kiss of Death will probably come for you, but if you're afraid of them, you can't conceive of the lengths I'd go through to keep you. Slash is nothing compared to me in any way, but especially not in something like this. He wants you because he has to assert his dominance. You left without his permission. He can't let that go or else he risks looking weak to his brothers." He paused then, looking straight into her eyes. The look she saw should have terrified her. It would have any sane woman. What she saw stamped into every line on his face, every sparkle in his eyes, was *possession*. Pure and simple. "You. Are. Mine."

"I won't be fair game for your club, Cain," she squeaked out. "I can't. I'm not like that."

His lips pulled back from his teeth in a snarl, and his arms tightened around her. He shoved inside her pussy until he was as deep as he could go, holding himself there until she gasped, digging her heels into his ass.

"*I do not share,*" he bit out. "My brothers know this."

"I'm sure they do, but --"

He cut her off. "*They know.* They'll respect my claim no matter what."

She held his gaze, some of the lust cut back to a simmer instead of a raging boil inside her. For a long while, neither of them spoke. He seemed to be waiting on her to acknowledge his statement. Angel tried to be realistic about the whole situation, but it was so surreal it was difficult. It all came down to trust. She didn't know him well enough to trust him, but looking into his eyes she knew one thing for certain: he absolutely believed what he was saying. The men in this club would not touch her if they thought he'd claimed her for his own.

"OK," she found herself whispering.

"We understand each other. No running. No other men."

She nodded. Angel needed to ask him if it went the other way with him and no women, but Cain began to... *move*.

Where up to this point Cain had been aggressive and borderline too rough, now he moved with slow, sensual twists of his hips. It was as if the need to be inside her had been driving his every thought, every action to this point. Once he was where he needed to be, he was more in control of himself and able to move things at the speed he wanted instead of what his body demanded. He finally raised himself above her on straightened arms and rolled his hips in quick little snaps a couple of times before rocking into her. Each time, he scraped her clit with his body, sending streaks of fire flicking through her.

She gasped, clinging to him, gripping his brawny arms as he fucked her. The muscles of his chest and abdomen rippled with every move he made. Never had Angel seen a more erotic sight than Cain's body moving to pleasure hers. And he was pleasuring her. He never took his eyes from hers. The man seemed to focus completely on her and her alone. It was an erotic enticement more compelling than anything in her life.

The second Angel felt the impending orgasm start and gasped out his name, Cain began a driving rhythm that seemed designed to take them both over the edge into insanity. Her body fragmented, pleasure exploding from within where his cock went deep. His bellow to the ceiling was as loud as her scream. Both of them locked their bodies, both of them clinging to each other. Cain had once again wrapped his arms tightly around her, holding her against him as he buried his face in her hair. Angel locked her ankles around his hips, grinding herself against him to draw out the lingering remains of bliss.

Finally, when they were both still, Cain rolled off her. He didn't let her go, but slid free of her body and pulled her on top of him so she lay half draped over him. Both were breathing heavily and sweat glistened off their skin. Angel wanted to lap at his chest, to catch those little beads with her tongue, but she didn't dare. Whatever this new relationship with Cain was, he'd define it. Not her. She wasn't stupid.

Several minutes later, Cain pulled the condom off his still semi-hard cock and knotted it, tossing it in the wastebasket beside the bed. He didn't get up, though. Instead, he pulled a quilt over them both and kissed her temple. That was the last thing Angel remembered before the steady beat of his heart lulled her to sleep.

Chapter Six

Cain woke when Angel whimpered beside him. She'd turned her back to him and was curled on her side, not touching him.

"Angel?" He rolled, putting his arms around her, pulling her stiff body against his. "What's wrong? You know you're safe with me."

"I'm fine," she gasped.

"No, you're not. Talk to me, Angel." It was an order. Nothing less. Cain didn't want to be harsh with her, but knowing she had a problem she refused to bring to him was maddening. It made him feel like he couldn't take care of his woman, no matter how little a time they'd been together.

She turned her head to look at him over her shoulder. Moonlight fell across her face, highlighting her features and expression, and he knew what her problem was.

"Ah," he said, relaxing. His cock did the opposite. Where he'd been semi-hard before, now blood rushed to fill him, readying him to pleasure his woman. "Turn over and look at me, baby." She complied, her eyes glazed with need. "If you need me, you take me. Understand?"

The puzzled look on her face told him she didn't, but Cain waited for her to speak. She needed to learn to tell him what was on her mind. He stroked her face with his thumb, silently encouraging her to confide in him.

She let loose a little sob, then blurted, "I *do* need you, Cain! I ache with it!"

"Listen to me, Angel baby. Look at me and really listen." He framed her face in his hands, forcing her to keep her gaze locked with his. "Anytime. Anywhere.

You need me, you take me. I don't care if it's the middle of the night, middle of the day, in the kitchen, on the lake, or -- if you're feeling particularly adventurous -- at a fucking party at the clubhouse. You need my body, it's yours."

"I wasn't sure how our relationship would work," she managed, but her hands had already gone to his chest, as if she'd just been waiting for permission. She stroked and traced every raised scar she could find as if starved to touch him. "I knew you'd lead it, but some men don't like women to initiate sex."

"Not me, baby. I'm up for it anytime you want it. Now. Tell me what you want to do to me."

There was the smallest relieved sigh from Angel as she sat up and tugged the covers from his body. Cain lay on his back, one hand stroking her back, the other behind his head.

"I want to touch you," she murmured. "Your body. All over. I've never seen a man like you and I want to... feel you. All your muscle and sinew. I love the way your body hair abrades my skin. I like knowing it's a man wrapped around me like you did when we first made love."

"Ah, baby. That's what I want to hear from you. Explore to your heart's content." Every word she spoke made his cock throb and ache even more. He'd bet he could get her to talk dirty to him with a minimal amount of encouragement.

She took her time, starting at his chest and running her hands over him. Finding his nipples and rubbing her palms over them until they stabbed into them. Then she trailed kisses over his chest, even flicking one nipple with her little tongue. It was impossible to hold back a groan when she did the other one.

Angel trailed her mouth over his abdomen, pausing only when she reached his cock. It stood out proud and pulsing under her gaze. When she looked back at him over her shoulder, he nodded his encouragement, and she took him in her small fist and then covered the head with the damp heat of her mouth.

Cain couldn't stop the explosion of sound from his throat, or the thrust of his hips up at her. His hand flew to her head and fisted in her hair. "Ah, Jesus, baby! Suck it hard! Fuck!"

She complied. At first she was tentative, but soon she was moving with sure, hard strokes of her mouth, pumping what she couldn't fit with her hand. His Angel took him deep. More than once he felt the back of her throat. It was all he could do not to hold her there, but managed. Until she held herself down for several seconds until she gagged on his length. Then all bets were off.

Cain thrust his hips at her, fucking her mouth as if he were fucking her cunt. Her fingers bit into his hips, actually urging him to thrust with little tugs. Over and over he thrust. Several times she gagged and he managed to pull back, but she always came back for more, worshiping his cock as if she'd been starved for him and him alone her entire life.

"Enough!" His roar startled her, and she jumped a little. He pulled her off him by her hair before snagging her around the waist and pulling her to the center of the bed. Rolling her over on her stomach, Cain pulled her hips up so she was on her knees. When she pushed up on her hands, he shoved her back so her head lay on the bed. "Ass up. Head down," he growled. "Going to fuck the shit out of you, woman!"

She whimpered, sweat slickening her delicate skin. Cain rolled a condom on and smacked one side of her ass in a sharp *smack*. Angel cried out, but rocked her hips from side to side as if she wanted more. So he obliged her on the other side.

"So fucking perfect," he said, rubbing his handprints. He could barely make them out in the moonlight, but knew they were there and that he'd put them there deliberately. "You tell me if I'm too rough. I swear I'll ease up if you say, but you have to say. Understand me, Angel?"

"I do," she panted. "Just fuck me, Cain. Please!"

Hearing his innocent Angel begging him to fuck her was all he could stand. Cain found her entrance slick and ready for him, which was a good thing because he needed inside her like he needed to breathe. One hard shove and he was enveloped by her. They both cried out.

Angel moved with him. He gripped her hips and pulled her back against him, but she followed his movements, urging him to ride her faster. Harder. She cried out, keeping her head on the bed like he'd asked, but using her arms to propel her body back into him as best as she could.

"You love this, don't you!" It wasn't a question.

"I do," she answered. "Love you fucking me so hard!"

"Fuck!"

Now that he had her talking, Cain was afraid he'd created a monster. She'd be his undoing, his singular match in the bedroom. She was submissive but demanding all the same. It was more of a turn-on then Cain would have thought possible.

"Gonna to fuck you hard, Angel," he grunted. "Gonna fuck you so fucking hard…"

"I'm coming!" She screamed out her release, her sheath milking him even as he tried to hold back just that little bit longer.

When she thrashed beneath him, Cain could take no more. He shoved her hips down and pressed his full weight on her, fucking her as hard as he could. Angel reached around and gripped his hips, digging in her nails and pulling him to her. She gasped and whimpered with every thrust of his cock, shrieking her pleasure again. This time, the pleasure was too much to hold back. With a brutal yell, he let himself go, coming harder than he had in living memory.

Once the last of the tremors left him he rolled them so they lay on their sides, holding her tightly against his chest. His cock was still deep inside her, and he was reluctant to lose that connection with her.

"Cain, that was wonderful."

"Did I hurt you?"

"No. Not at all. It was…" She giggled. "It was fun. So much fun."

He swatted her ass lightly as he pulled out of her and disposed of the condom. "Wench." He moved them back to the pillows and covered them both with the quilts. Once he had her settled against him, her hand resting on his chest, her head on his shoulder, he sighed. Cain was more contented than he could ever remember being.

"Anytime you need me, baby. Anytime."

"I'll keep that in mind," she said, her voice drowsy.

"Good. It goes both ways. I'll be taking you when I need you too."

He felt her smile against him. "See that you do."

It was a long time before Cain finally dozed off. When he woke, he knew what he was going to do. No sense half-doing anything. He'd force Angel into his world and see how she fared. If she was miserable, if he couldn't make her happy and find a place for her she could live with, he'd let her go.

Who the fuck was he kidding? He'd never let her go. Didn't think he was capable of it. Not since he'd had her. Angel was like no woman he'd ever met before. She was innocence and sin rolled into one. She responded to him unlike any other lover he'd taken and was genuine about it. He'd looked into her eyes when he'd taken her. She'd been as lost as he'd been. No. He wouldn't let her go. So that left only one option.

But how to make her happy here? With his club?

Carefully, he extracted himself from her arms in the early morning light. He didn't want to wake her yet. Not until he'd had time to form a plan of attack. First things first, though. He needed to talk to Mama and Pops. They would be imperative in winning her over.

God, but she was beautiful! Long hair black as a raven's wing. As the sun filtered through the curtain, little blue highlights wove within the curls. During the night, he remembered that lovely hair twining around them both, tangling them together. Her eyes, expressive and wide with wonder, were like the richest amber. He'd known she was trouble the first moment he'd laid eyes on her. Trouble for him. For a battle-hardened man like him, conceding defeat to a small woman was intolerable.

Except it wasn't.

The pleasure he'd found in her body was nothing short of cataclysmic. She'd altered his life from the moment he'd seen her, but now he had to figure out how to secure her to him.

Cain turned his back on her, padding downstairs to the phone. He called Mama and set up a time for both him and Angel to meet with her. Then he and his brothers would plan what to do when Slash came for her.

He was working that over in his mind when his phone rang.

"Yeah," he said in greeting.

"We've got maybe a day -- if that -- before someone from Kiss of Death approaches us," Torpedo said with no embellishment. "Someone tipped them off. Data says someone close to us. Probably inside the club."

"He say who?" It was all Cain could do not to voice a denial. Someone inside the club? Betraying their brothers? There was no one he didn't trust completely. Every single one of them had been together for years either in the military or with ExFil, the independent contracting company he owned. They ran protection detail overseas for government officials of several nations. Bones took on anyone who could pay and needed their services. Bottom line, they'd had each other's backs in the worst of circumstances and where the only people they knew for a fact they could rely on were each other. No way had one of them betrayed the club in this manner.

"He said he had an idea. He also said not to lose your cool. It was all good."

"Really. It's all good. Someone leads the fuckin' enemy to our fuckin' door, and it's all good?"

"He said he'd give you an answer by the time you made it to the clubhouse." Torpedo didn't sound concerned. Probably no one else could pick up on the little nuances of his moods, but Cain could. The rest of his brothers as well. So damned many years together made that possible. One more thing he had to consider with Angel. He was several years older than she was. It was just too damned much to worry about right now, especially with the threat approaching them and, possibly, the one inside his own club.

"He'd better. And there better be a good fuckin' reason or I may kill someone tonight."

"Just get over here with your woman. Bohannon is waiting for you at the end of your driveway."

"I don't need babysittin'." Not that it would do any good to tell the other man that. As vice president of the club, Torpedo had the right to put men on him if he thought it was necessary.

"I'm aware of that. You're as lethal as any of us. But with Kiss of Death out there, as well as Scars and Bars, I'm not taking any chances. You'll protect Angel if you're attacked and leave yourself vulnerable."

"I can take care of myself *and* her."

"I know. Bohannon is still waiting at the end of the drive. Goose and Dead Eye got you from a distance."

With an angry stab of his thumb, Cain disconnected the call. "Fucker," he muttered. He hadn't really expected anything different, but he still didn't like it. Dead Eye was the team's sniper. Goose was his spotter. The two had been inseparable since they'd been assigned together. Having those two on him meant Bohannon was spooked and in full protection mode. He could only imagine how he had their clubhouse locked down.

With an oath, he tossed the phone across the room. It bounced harmlessly on a chair. Not nearly as satisfying as if it had gone through the window or shattered against the wall, but probably for the best. If Bohannon had tried to call him and Cain hadn't answered, there would have been hell to pay. He hated not having time to ease Angel into this. Making love to her all night was one thing, but she wasn't ready for a commitment. The best he could hope for was to have her turn to him for her protection.

"Cain?"

He looked up and his heart melted just a little. She stood on the landing, the sheet from their bed wrapped around her. One small hand clutched it tightly to her chest as she gazed down at him. Those lovely amber eyes were wide with trepidation. All that glorious hair fell around her to her waist like a dark cloud, making her look small and vulnerable.

"We need to go back the clubhouse," he told her.

"I thought we were staying here a while."

"I know. I'm sorry. There's been a change in circumstances, and Bohannon has requested us back where we can better defend ourselves if needed. He likes us all in one place, and I don't like the idea of anyone knowing where my house is outside the club."

"By anyone, do you mean Slash and Kiss of Death?"

He shrugged, trying to be casual about it. "We'll have an escort back to the clubhouse. Once there, you can go to my room and rest if you want."

"What about the children?"

"Mama and Pops will bring them as well. They're in our circle of protection just like you are."

She didn't say anything for a long moment, looking down at him intently, probably trying to gauge the truth. Finally, she nodded and turned to go to her room to dress. Cain wished he'd brought her things to his bedroom so it would be *their* bedroom. He'd never shared a personal space with a woman. Just one more thing about his life he was dying to change for her. God, he was in so much trouble!

Ten minutes later, they were on the road, Bohannon, Sword, and Trucker flanking them. Cain looked up on the ridge above the winding road to his lakeside home. Sure enough, Dead Eye and Goose were above them, keeping them safe from a distance. His brothers. Having his back. They always had, and he was confident they always would. Now they had one more person to protect.

They rolled in through the fence surrounding the property. The second they were through, the two prospects waiting inside slid the gate shut before going back to their posts in the trees. Two more prospects stood guard on top of the clubhouse.

Cain parked, helping Angel to her feet. He urged her inside and led her to his room.

"Rest. I'll come for you later."

"You're not sending me to my room like I'm a naughty child, Cain," she said, sticking her chin up defiantly. "I'm a big girl."

He grinned at her, unable to resist bending his head and taking her mouth briefly. "I know, Angel. No one is making you stay here. You can come with me to the great room if you want. I think the children are already there."

"Good. I'll stay with them. An abrupt change in routine might frighten them."

"They're strong kids, baby. Don't worry so much about them."

"Someone needs to, Cain. I have no idea what happened to them, but I know without a doubt they've been through something bad."

"I know. Suzie needs someone fussing over her from time to time. Daniel and Cliff, however, need to feel like they're taken seriously as men. They're young yet, but they still need to feel as independent as they can."

"They look out for her, you know. Protect her. They're very good at it, too."

"They're good young men."

He and Angel stepped into the great room. All the club members were there, including Mama, Pops, and the kids. A couple of prospects lingered by the door, but took a cue from Bohannon, nodded at the other man, then stepped outside, closing the door behind them.

"Everyone OK?" Torpedo looked to Cain.

"Why wouldn't we be?" he shrugged.

Bohannon raised an eyebrow, giving him and Torpedo a look before taking a seat. No one said anything for a while. Sober faces looked at Cain, waiting for him to speak. Looking around the room, he didn't see even one face he didn't trust with his life. So who was their traitor?

Before he had to say anything, Data cleared his throat. "I think we can all relax," he said. "Cain, you know I wouldn't say that lightly."

Cain did know. "I understand. Threat contained?"

Data shrugged. "Mostly. As much as it can be, anyway. Slash is still coming, and I think with a few of his trusted men, but everything else is... fine. Understandable even."

So, whoever betrayed them had a reason. Didn't mean there wouldn't be consequences. Just meant they got to live.

"We're out of time," Bohannon said, meeting Cain's gaze directly. So, Kiss of Death was on the way now. For some reason, Bohannon didn't want to come out and say it, so Cain didn't either. He met the other man's gaze and was surprised to see the man flick a glance where the children and Angel had huddled together before looking back at Cain. So, Angel? No. He didn't believe that. Which left only the children...

Cain cocked his head, ready to ask Bohannon what the hell he meant when one of the prospects, Clutch, opened the door. He didn't say a word, just stuck his head in and found Bohannon's gaze, nodding once.

Every member of the team reached for a weapon. They were silent except for the metallic slide-clicks of guns all over the room as each man chambered a round. Moments later, three large men in patched Kiss of Death leathers entered. Moments after that, their president followed.

Slash was deceptively short, but stocky and heavily muscled. His head was balding, and he'd taken to shaving it. Dark, hawk-like eyes peered around the room, though he was careful to keep behind his men. He might be showing balls the size of Texas coming into another club's house intending to demand something from them, but he wasn't completely stupid. Just... uninformed. He had no idea who he was dealing with.

"Slash, I presume." Cain kept his voice congenial but didn't move to greet the other man with a handshake. "President of Kiss of Death?"

"I am. You know who I am. Do you know why I'm here?"

"If I knew for sure, you'd already be dead." Cain didn't pull his punches. He wanted the other men to know what they'd walked into. Mainly so that, when it all went to shit, he could say he gave them every opportunity to back out gracefully. The only reason he did that was for Angel's benefit. He didn't want her to see him as a cold-blooded killer, even if he could be when necessary. "Why don't I hear it from your own mouth?"

Slash lifted one corner of his mouth. "I'd heard you were a cocky bastard. I guess that's true."

"Cocky may or may not be able to back it up."

"I'm assuming you think you can?"

That irritated Cain. Surely this guy had done his homework before going deep in enemy territory. "Do you really want a rundown? I'd have thought you'd look into that before making the ride all this way."

Slash shrugged. "I did. I guess I just want to hear it, as you say, from your own mouth." His grin was evil. What was his game?

Cain glanced at Torpedo and Bohannon. Both men were on alert. He knew Bohannon had a direct link to the team guarding the house, as well as the prospects assigned to help. The enforcer's face was hard, displeased in the extreme. He nodded, indicating there was no immediate threat, but to be alert. Apparently, Slash had brought more than he was showing. Not unexpected. He was stalling.

"Very well. We're all former Special Forces. We're the people the CIA hires when they can't take official action. Each of us have more *sanctioned* kills than your entire club has on the down-low. In short, none of us would hesitate to kill you for looking at

Angel in a way we don't much like. And we have anything and everything we need to wage an all-out war with any dumb fuck crossing our path." He finished by resting his hand on the gun at his hip. "Anything else you want to hear straight from me?"

The man looked a touch wary now, but didn't back down. "She's ours," he said, indicating Angel. "So's the little brat. You can have the boys if you want them. We just want the girls."

Cain raised an eyebrow but said nothing.

"Give us the kid, and we'll call it even."

"No." Cain didn't hesitate. Behind him, Suzie whimpered softly, but kept silent otherwise. "Angel's my old lady, and Suzie and the boys will soon be ours legally."

Slash's face darkened. "You can't take property from another club. I already own both those bitches."

"Then we have nothing more to discuss."

The second the words left Cain's mouth, Bohannon and Torpedo lunged for the two men near them. Cain was focused on Slash, who deftly dodged the fight to move deeper into the room. No doubt, he was going for the girls. A quick glance in their direction showed the two teenage boys shepherding Angel and Suzie as far back in the room as they could. The boys crouched down, ready to attack if anyone got too close. They looked wild, almost feral, lips peeled back from their teeth. Those boys looked as dangerous as any of the Bones members.

Cain made a lunging dive for Slash, tackling him and landing two quick punches to the man's gut. The satisfying grunt as the breath left Slash's lungs told him he'd hit his mark. There was a vague impression of fights going on around him, but Cain's focus was on Slash as the man tried to kick himself free.

There was a flash of a gun, and Cain's breath caught. Slash had pulled free his weapon and was taking aim at the group of kids and Angel where they huddled in the corner of the room.

Chapter Seven

Angel saw the gun. Knew Slash was going to kill them. Suzie didn't scream. It might have been better if she had. The little girl clung to her, burying her face against Angel and whimpering softly. The boys had put themselves in front of her and Suzie like a solid wall, prepared to take the brunt of the attack.

"No!" she screamed, shoving Suzie away from her and back into the wall. Angel fought to get in front of the boys, to push them behind her to protect the little girl. She desperately wanted them away from what she saw as the front line.

Cain managed to roll Slash over so that his aim was off. Thank God, too, because the gun went off with a deafening bellow, the bullet burying itself in the wall not two feet from little Suzie.

"Bastard!" Angel screamed, throwing herself into the fight, needing to get the gun away from Slash. Cain had wrapped his legs around Slash's middle from behind, locking them at the ankles. He had Slash's gun hand over his head with Cain's arm locked around Slash's in some kind of complicated hold, preventing another shot. Slash still had his finger on the trigger, though, putting the other members of the club and his own men in just as much danger.

All she had was her fists to fight with. She was a small woman and wasn't sure how much good it would do her, but she swung with her right hand as hard as she could into Slash's face.

Just like that, all the fear and resulting rage came back to her. One blow turned to two. Then four. Then she turned over on her butt and kicked him in the face. Over and over she rained blows on Slash, needing to hurt him like his club had hurt her. Like he would have hurt her. He would have killed her. Would have killed the children she taught and had grown to love and respect. Little Suzie had been terrified from the moment the man had entered, as if she instinctively knew he was there to hurt her. For every woman who had ever been brutalized by this kind of man, she beat and kicked and *punished* Slash.

It was a long while later when Cain let him go. Angel was still pounding a bloodied and beaten Slash when Cain and Torpedo pulled her off him. Slash didn't move, his breath coming in a sickening rattle.

"That's enough, baby," Cain soothed as he gently wrapped his arms around her, turning her away from the bloody mess. He urged her to look up at him as he pulled her closer, his strong arms securely locking her to him. Slowly, she became aware of everything around her. Cain's strength. The absolute quiet, other than Slash's labored breathing. The scent of blood and gun smoke.

The intense turquoise of Cain's eyes...

Then she dissolved into tears, her legs giving out. Cain held her against him securely, not even a hint he'd drop her. Instead, he scooped her up to carry her through the clubhouse.

"Suzie. Bring Cliff and Daniel with you and come with us," Cain commanded. Distantly, Angel recognized he hadn't said simply, "Kids," but used their names. Vaguely, she wondered if that was a gesture of respect. The boys, after all, had proven they were men by protecting her and Suzie.

Angel didn't know if they followed or not. She couldn't think. Couldn't concentrate on anything other than Cain and his strength and clean smell and the taste of his sweat where her lips pressed against his neck. Her mind seemed to cling to these things.

Probably to cancel out everything from the common room and what she'd done.

"Oh, God," she whispered. "Oh, God. Oh, God!"

"Shhh, baby," Cain soothed. "Everything's fine. You're safe, and so is everyone else."

"Did I... did I kill him?"

"No," he said without hesitation. "You didn't." He was so quick with the denial, she had to wonder. Angel thought about that for a minute. Could she live with herself if she had killed Slash?

Yes. She might have nightmares, but she'd been saving herself and the children, not to mention the other members of the club. Anyone could have been shot if she hadn't done what she'd done.

Cain sat her down on an exam table, and Angel looked at her hands. Blood was splattered up her arms. Her hands hurt where she'd pounded them into Slash's face. She vaguely remembered it was why she'd scooted back to use her feet, kicking out, her boots connecting with his body and face. The pain for her had been less. The damage to Slash worse. At the time, she hadn't really registered anything other than the need to hurt the man.

Mama took her hands and examined them, gently wiping off the blood with a damp cloth. "I'll need to clean and disinfect the cuts, dear. It might sting a little, but I'll be as gentle as I can."

"I'm all right," Angel whispered. "Do what you have to."

It stung, but not badly. It was easier to look at her hands once Mama had washed all the blood off. She could almost forget what she'd done. Then she flexed her fingers, and they ached. A fresh wave of tears threatened, but she bit her lip, determined to suck it up. She'd shown enough weakness in front of these people.

"Miss Angel," Suzie said, her voice wavering. Angel looked up, meeting Suzie's gaze. The girl's lip was trembling, and tears glistened in her eyes. Angel slid from the table and wrapped her arms around Suzie while they both wept. Daniel and Cliff both joined them, crying just as hard as her and Suzie. Angel put her arms around all three as best she could, doing her best to comfort all three children.

"Everyone's OK now," she said over and over. She needed to reinforce that to them. They *were* all going to be fine. They'd make it through this together. She wasn't going anywhere, and they were safe.

"I'm so sorry, Miss Angel," Daniel finally said. "This was all our fault."

"Honey, there was no way you could have prevented this. Slash was coming after me no matter what."

"You don't understand," Cliff said, rubbing at his eyes and wiping his nose with the back of his sleeve. "We told them where you were. Me and Daniel."

"I knew it, too," Suzie said quietly, still clinging to Angel. "We thought..." She paused, sobbing.

"We thought Bones would kill them," Daniel said, his voice wavering as he spoke. "We wanted Bones to *have* to kill them."

"What?" Angel didn't let go of Suzie, but knew her eyes were wide with shock when she faced the young man.

Both Daniel and Cliff hung their heads in shame and backed away from her. Finally, Daniel looked up at her, then to Mama and Cain. "We're sorry we got Angel in trouble, but we're not sorry if you killed them," he qualified, looking straight at Cain. "They was bad people."

Cain didn't answer, but nodded once at the boy.

Cliff took a breath. "We were with them before we came here," he said. "They were mean to Suzie. Tried to get us to be mean to her, too. She's too little to do what they..." He trailed off before turning and fleeing from the room. Out in the hall, Angel heard him retching and sobbing. Daniel looked as pale as Cliff, but managed to hold his own.

"We know," Cain finally said. "Data got it all before Slash and his men got here. They were hunting all of you as well."

"Mostly just Suzie," Daniel muttered. "They were so mean to her."

"She's safe now. So are you and Cliff."

The young man looked equal parts relieved and disbelieving. "You ain't gonna kick us out for betraying you guys?"

"No," he said. "But I hope you've learned to come to us instead of taking matters into your own hands. This could have just as easily turned into a bloodbath."

"We didn't exactly think it all the way through, I guess," Daniel acknowledged. "We knew Miss Angel ran from Gremlin because we was there right after she left. They had pictures of her up all over the place so everyone would recognize her. When we got here and she showed up, we figured if Bones had to defend themselves to keep Angel away from Kiss of Death, we'd be safe too. Hopefully forever."

"I meant what I said." Cain glanced at Daniel and Suzie before settling on Angel. "Angel and I are going to adopt all three of you."

Daniel looked excited, and then his face fell. "If you do that, we'll be in the system. They'll take us away before it even gets started."

"You leave that to me," he said. "Just like with Kiss of Death, I've got your back."

Angel wanted to protest, but found she couldn't. He was not only making a promise to the kids, he was making a promise to her.

"We'll talk about this later," she said, lowering her own gaze. If she continued to stare into his eyes, she'd believe anything he told her. Hell, she'd just met him! Why would he even contemplate any kind of relationship with her other than sexual? Adopting three children implied marriage. While the concept of an old lady implied at least a long-term relationship, he'd said nothing about marriage.

And why would she even want him to? They'd had sex. Sure. Sex didn't mean they were in it for the long haul. Or even a short haul!

Cain chuckled, shaking his head as he took her hand and kissed the palm. "You're not talking yourself out of this before we even have a chance to discuss it," he said.

"Why not? Sounds like you've talked yourself *into* it before we've talked."

He grinned. "Yep." And took her hand. "Mama, let me know if they need anything. Angel and I need to work this out."

"Does that mean you're not adopting us?" Suzie's lower lip trembled. "I guess you don't want us after this, huh?"

"That's not it at all, baby," Angel said. She tried to pull away from Cain to reassure the little girl, but he wouldn't let her go. "Cain and I haven't known each other that long. But I promise we'll figure out some way to keep you legally. I don't know how yet, but we will. You'll never have to leave until you're ready." When Suzie dropped her head, slumping in defeat, she knew the child wasn't buying it but didn't say anything else.

"Don't worry, Suzie. I'll change her mind." When the child looked up, he winked at her, and she smiled back at him before turning to look at Angel. Probably for reassurance.

Exasperated, Angel rolled her eyes. "We'll talk about it," she affirmed. "*Talk*."

"We'll do a hell of a lot more than talk," he said in her hair, his lips tickling her ear sensually. "Come with me."

* * *

Other than making love with Angel, Cain thought there was nothing quite like the feeling of flying down an open stretch of road on his bike. The Night Train Harley was a smooth ride and, with Angel clinging to him so sweetly from behind, Cain was sure he was as close to heaven as he could be. Other than when in bed with Angel in his arms. They were going back to his home, eventually, but he wanted to take her riding for a while. It always mellowed him out. He saw no reason it wouldn't do the same for her.

When they'd first started out, she'd been stiff, trying to hold herself away from him. As they'd continued down the road, she'd relaxed until she'd finally laid her face against his back and nuzzled him. He'd patted her hand affectionately, praising her.

The sun was bright and warm. The day clear. The air fresh. His Harley purred contentedly at the extended ride, as if it had merely been waiting for the chance to soar down the highway.

He took her on a giant circle across two counties for more than two hours before they finally pulled into his driveway. Even when he put the kickstand down and turned off the bike, neither of them got off immediately.

"That was wonderful," she said, her voice content as she rubbed her face against his back. "I've never ridden like that. In fact, the only time I've ever been on a bike was when you brought me here before, and then took me back to the clubhouse."

"It won't be the last time, Angel," he promised. "Let's go inside." He urged her off before dismounting himself, needing to have her in his arms. Needing *her*.

"Cain," she started before taking a step away, trying to put space between them.

"No, Angel," he said, matching her step so she was still near. "We're going inside. I'm going to make love to you and convince you to be my old lady. If you aren't ready for marriage just yet, I'll work on you until you are. No matter how long it takes. Understand me, though. Me claiming you as my old lady seals the deal for me. I'll marry you because I know you need it. Not because I consider it 'more' than me putting my property patch on your jacket."

"You don't even know me," she protested, but didn't keep any distance between them. "How could you possibly know you want to marry me? Marriage is something I take very seriously. I don't intend to get divorced once I commit my life to someone else, so I don't intend to get married until I'm sure."

"I'll make you happy, baby," he assured. "I'll make you so happy you can't even imagine leaving me."

"And what if you get tired of *me*? You're the one rushing us into this."

He grinned and pulled her into his arms. "Then keep me happy, too. Distract me with sex so much I can't imagine what I'd do without you."

She giggled in spite of her misgivings. "You're horrible."

Cain scooped her up, carrying her inside the house. "I'm serious," he said, grinning at her as he set her on her feet, gripping her shoulders and looking straight into her eyes. Cain wanted with everything in him for her to see he meant what he was saying. "I don't know how or why, but you got to me, Angel. Your compassion with the kids. Your willingness to help them, to care about what's best for them despite how much you needed the job of being their teacher, proved that. You took the time to recognize their intelligence, their insecurities, and their protectiveness of each other. You also braved talking to me so I'd be aware of what you saw as limitations on your part." He shuddered as he thought about what her ass looked like when he'd admired it as she bent over one of the kids, the prim and proper schoolmarm. "And you're so Goddamned sexy in those fuckin' skirts of yours I can't breathe when I see your ass in them. Makes me want to peel them off you and fuck you until neither of us can stand."

Angel gasped, her hands flying to his chest where her fingers curled into the muscles there. He loved that she clung to him like he was hers. Loved that she blushed when he talked dirty to her. He tilted her face up to his with his thumb, looking into those lovely dark eyes, held her gaze for a few moments, and then lowered his mouth to hers.

Cain was amazed at how instantly he reacted to her touch. It was almost visceral and so intense he could almost convince himself she'd actually cast a spell over him. She was so soft and fresh. Innocent. Yet not. The combination drove him crazy and drew him like a fly to honey all at the same time. Her tongue darted out to meet his boldly, her little whimpers and moans growing with each second as she grew as desperate for him as he was for her.

Finally, needing her so badly he couldn't wait any longer, he carried her to his bedroom -- now their bedroom. Deliberately, he backed away from her to remove his clothes and was happy when she followed suit. His Angel didn't play coy or act as if she wasn't sure about this, she simply stood in front of him, naked. Her breasts were high and proud, dark nipples puckered in the slight breeze from the open window.

"You scared the shit out of me when I realized you'd jumped into the fight, Angel. I saw you, and I knew I never wanted violence to ever touch you." He reached for her, and Angel floated into his arms. Her slim arms circled his neck, her fingers threading through the hair at his neck.

"I saw the gun," she whispered. "Saw Slash pointing it at me and the children. I didn't want them hurt. Couldn't bear the thought of that ugliness touching or harming them."

"So you threw yourself into the fight to protect them."

"And you," she whispered. "I... I don't think I could stand it if something happened to you, and I don't understand why. I barely know you."

"You feel it too," he said, urging her to look at him once more. "You're supposed to be with me."

"Maybe," she said, grinning. "Or maybe you're supposed to be with me."

Cain couldn't help but chuckle. "Maybe I am," he agreed. "As long as we're together, I don't suppose the semantics make much of a difference." He stared into her eyes for long, long moments. "You good?"

"I will be," she said. "As soon as you take me to bed."

"With pleasure."

Lifting the woman of his dreams into his arms, Cain laid her on the bed and covered her with his larger frame. He speared his fingers through her hair, letting the dark strands tangle around him like a silken bond. In a way, he supposed he was bound to her. He was a warrior, needing no one but his brothers. Until Angel Black had come into his life. Now, he needed her like he needed air. She was... precious to him, worthy of his protection and that of his brothers. Looking at her now, he was struck by how determined he was to protect and cherish her.

To love her.

Cain trailed kisses down her body, pausing at her belly button to swirl his tongue there. She giggled, her hand going to his head. He looked up at her and nipped the flesh beneath her navel gently. Her breath caught, the smile vanishing instantly. He smirked.

The flesh between her legs was wet and weeping. Cain stroked gently with his fingers, wetting them, then rubbing her clit in little circles. Angel's cries spurred him on, letting him know what she wanted. She seemed to hold her breath as he hovered over her pussy, blowing gently over her fevered flesh.

Another gentle rush of fluid from her, and Cain could wait no more. With his own ragged groan, he dipped his head to her pussy and drank. He sucked her lips, lashing them with his tongue before letting each go with a gentle pop. Her clit was swollen and nearly throbbed under his gaze, begging for his tongue, lips, and teeth. He obliged.

When she was shrieking and writhing under him, begging him to fuck her, Cain crawled up her body and thrust into her. Her legs locked around him, her heels digging into his ass. She dug in, urging him to move faster. Harder. When she got impatient with him, she simply lifted herself to meet his thrusts.

Slim arms and legs wrapped around him, Angel tried to take over the pace Cain had set. He let her, to a point, but he didn't want her to climax until he had her mindless.

"You want to come?" he growled in her ear.

"Yes! Please!" Her little plea was the sweetest music.

"You wait until I tell you."

"Cain! God!"

He slammed into her several times before holding himself as deep as he could go, his body mashed against hers, buried deep inside her. "Look at me," he growled. "Open your eyes and look into mine."

She took several breaths, her pussy contracting around his cock. Her muscles tempted him, trying to make him come before he was ready. Cain bit his cheek to keep from giving in. Not yet. Not until she knew she was his.

Finally, she opened her eyes, gazing up into his with wonder and dismay. He licked her lips once, still holding her gaze. "You see now," he whispered. "We belong together. You. Me. We'll give those children a home. Someplace they know they will always be safe."

For a long time, Angel said nothing. Then she nodded slowly. Her smile, when it came, was brilliant, her eyes seeming to glow with happiness. "Yes, Cain. I think that's a very good idea."

He kissed her then, pouring all the longing, lust, and budding love he had for her into that kiss. As he kissed her, he started to move again.

Building...

Building...

Her pussy gripped him, her muscles rippling as she fought off her orgasm. He waited a couple more moments and then commanded, "Come, Angel. Come on my cock and scream my name."

She did. More than once.

When the pleasure waned for her, Cain let himself go, his own orgasm overtaking him like a tidal wave. He arched his back and bellowed as his cock ejaculated hot cum inside her. The pleasure was inconceivable. Nothing in his life had ever prepared him for something as soul-searing as this. As his very essence emptied into Angel, he knew he'd given an important part of himself to her in that moment. He could see in her eyes she'd given a part of herself to him as well.

Both of them lay there, the weight of the moment oddly freeing to Cain. When her hand came up to caress his cheek, an expression of awe on her lovely face, Cain knew she felt the same.

"I never thought myself capable of love, Angel," he said, not exactly sure what he was going to say but needing to work it out before the moment was lost. "But I'm falling hard for you. It's more than possession or lust." He stroked her face, kissing her gently before continuing. "You're... special."

She smiled. "That's right," she said softly. "And don't you forget it."

"I have something for you." Giving her another soft kiss, Cain rolled off her. He crossed the room to his closet where he removed the plastic from a jacket there.

With the garment in his hands, Cain returned and handed it to her.

He found himself holding his breath as she examined it. On the back was the Bones insignia. The top rocker -- the curved patch at the top -- read "Property of," and the bottom rocker held "Cain." His club colors. His name. Cain found himself holding his breath.

Angel looked up at him. "You're giving me this? When did you do this?"

He shrugged as if it were no big deal. But it was. At least it was to him. "Not long after you started here. I knew I'd give it to you even as I promised myself I wouldn't."

"You seriously want me to wear this?" She looked up at him, her eyes wide. Cain's heart fell. Yeah, the property thing was a bit much for someone not used to the biker lifestyle, but it meant everything in his world. It was the one thing he could do to keep her protected even when he wasn't with her. That jacket proclaimed her off limits because he was her man. Anyone who knew him -- and he wasn't exactly the type to hide from other MCs -- would honor his claim either out of respect or fear. Either was fine so long as Angel was safe.

"It's not as bad as it sounds." He hated being on the defensive, but this was what she'd driven him to.

"No! It's not that. I know what it means. I just... are you sure this is what you want? I know it's a big deal in a club. If it's just to keep me with you, know that I'm staying as long as we're an exclusive couple. I don't do casual sex."

He laughed. "I'm actually disturbed at how relieved I am you said that."

"Pardon me for saying, but you don't seem like a one-woman kind of man. We haven't really discussed this part. I get that you expect me to be with you alone, but what about you?"

He wrapped his arms around her. It just felt right having her there. Finally he admitted, "I'm not a one-woman kind of man." When she huffed and punched him, Cain laughed and added, "At least, I wasn't." He pulled back to frame her face with his hands. "I am now. There will never be another woman for me. Even if I lose you. Which I absolutely will *not do*."

"Then I'll wear your patch. Wear it proudly." Her smile was radiant. Lovely as the morning.

"You're so... *beautiful*," he whispered. "My old lady."

She giggled. "I never thought I'd like the sound of that. When it comes from you, I could get used to it."

Bohannon (Bones MC 2)

Marteeka Karland

Luna: Never in a million years did I think I'd meet up with my childhood hero like this. Beaten down and scared out of my mind, my heart dropped when I realized who had me. I've never been so humiliated in my life, but Gage Bohannon the man is even harder to resist than the ridiculous fantasy I'd held on to.

Bohannon: I've never kept a woman who didn't want to be kept. But I've made more than one good girl turn rogue. If I had any decency in me at all, I'd have locked her in my room and left her alone. Instead, I'll take whatever she wants to give me and coax a few things she doesn't.

Chapter One

Driving the beat-up Ford down the dusty one-lane road at two in the morning was the last place Luna expected to find herself. If she made it out of this without being thrown in prison -- or killed -- she might just kill her brother. Markus had gotten her into this mess with his drug habit and debt. She had a soft heart for her brother, so here she was.

The night seemed to mock her. It was the perfect summer night. A soft breeze under a cloudless sky with stars everywhere. A crescent moon shone above, a golden contrast to the silvery stars. It was cool enough to be comfortable in the humid Kentucky summer, but warm enough she wasn't damp and cold with the windows of the truck down. Honeysuckle still permeated the air in places. Had she not been in the position she was in, she would have sighed with contentment.

"Quarter mile out." The CB radio next to her startled Luna so bad, she squealed. That was her signal to turn off her headlights and turn on her emergency flashers. If her brother had been in the truck next to her, she would have shoved him out and made him walk back to town. If she got out of this, she was seriously redefining their relationship.

Without the benefit of headlights, Luna had to go slow. Slower than she was sure the people she was meeting would like. But, damn it, she didn't know the road! Didn't have the first idea where she was or how to get out other than the little dirt path she was presently running. Naturally, her first -- and hopefully only -- drug run had to be in completely unfamiliar territory.

Two minutes later, she saw five shadowy figures emerge from the tree line. Another cue. This time, she was to turn off the flashers and kill the motor. She did so, trembling as she placed her hands on top of the steering wheel, gripping the thing in a white-knuckled hold.

Three of the five approached her. Two on her side, one on the passenger's side. All of them wore ski masks.

"Eyes forward," one of them snapped. "Keep your hands on the wheel." They'd told Luna this repeatedly before she'd left. Under no circumstances was she to remove her hands from the top of the steering wheel. If she did, they'd shoot her.

She closed her eyes tightly, willing herself to stay absolutely still. Not to look at her surroundings or the people outside the vehicle. Just a few more minutes and it would all be over. It was her mantra. Like a child trying to get through an unpleasant ordeal. Once done she could go home, take a hot bath, and fall apart where no one could witness.

There was rattling in the truck's bed as they unlocked the toolboxes and dug around for their "product." She had no idea exactly what she was hauling, but suspected it was pot or meth. Or both. Probably some kind of opioid 'cause, you know, might as well contribute to *that* problem, too.

Two of the three carried their take back to the two waiting at the tree line while the last of the five men kept a steady eye on her, a gun aimed loosely at her. Without meaning to, she let her eyes open and her head automatically turned to the window. Her gaze instantly fell on the beady eyes of the man guarding her. He fixed his gaze on her, making her skin crawl. Immediately, she regretted her action. Especially when he shoved the barrel of his gun sharply against her temple, forcing her head back around to face forward.

"I said eyes forward, bitch," he snapped.

There was muffled talk around her, and she realized there were probably more men than she'd originally seen. Which meant she was in even deeper shit than she suspected. To make matters worse, their voices were rising in anger with every second.

"You said there'd be twice as much smack! I can't take this back to Handlebar! He would have my balls, and I wouldn't blame him!"

"There should *be* twice as much. I'm going on what Poacher said to expect yesterday. Something must have happened."

"Something happened, all right," the guy snapped. "I'm getting cheated's what happened!" He raised his voice and spoke to someone out of her field of vision. "Check the rest of it! If we're being fucked, I'll kill every motherfucker here from this piece of shit club!"

"Poacher would never risk a war with another club. Especially not here."

"Don't much care what that bastard would risk. He cheated us, he'll get a war whether or not he wants one!"

"You don't understand." The guy continued to plead his case. "This is Bones territory. If a war starts here, Bones will kill everyone involved just to prove a point."

"They can try. Crow gave me orders, and he's not much scared of anyone so I follow orders no matter whose fucking territory I'm in."

Luna squeezed her eyes shut. Sweat trickled down her neck and between her breasts. There was a very good chance she wasn't getting out of here alive.

Prayers she hadn't uttered since she was a young child fell from her lips in a whispered mantra.

"There's half of what we were expecting," a guy called from the back of the truck. "Who do you want me to kill first?"

Luna knew she needed to keep her head forward, but she couldn't help but finally open her eyes and glance at the men arguing so close to her.

"Now wait just a Goddamned minute!"

Before the Scars and Bars member could say anything else, a gunshot rang out. A hole blossomed in the center of his forehead, and he collapsed to the ground. Luna was so scared she couldn't even whimper, knowing death was seconds away. The steel of the gun barrel was hot like a branding iron against her temple. She could almost feel the man holding the gun on her squeezing the trigger...

Another shot rang out. The hand holding the gun on her dropped into the truck with her -- along with the gun it held -- in a hot spray of blood. The guy let out a startled scream that probably had little to do with the sudden trauma and everything to do with the shock of it. Whoever was shooting at them meant business. That had to be one big ass gun to shoot a man's hand off with a single shot.

All around her, men yelled and shot wildly into the wooded night. She knew better than to move even though her every instinct screamed at her to get the fuck out of there. There was no way of knowing who the new threat was, but they weren't members of Scars and Bars or the other club. With every shot, with every man who dropped, Luna felt her own death looming. The worst part wasn't knowing she would die. She'd accepted that when she agreed to do this job for Markus. No. The worst part was knowing every shot that didn't take her down was a temporary stay of execution. It was torture unlike anything she'd ever imagined.

As suddenly as the fight had begun, it ceased. An eerie hush fell over the night, which was oddly peaceful. If not for the stench of blood all around her. Including on her person. Somewhere in the truck was a bloody hand clenching a gun. Luna wanted to get out of the vehicle and run into the woods where no one could find her. Except she had the feeling whoever had just executed these men was at home in the woods.

On cue, several shadowy figures appeared, rifles in hand, moving like a military unit. They checked every body they came upon, sometimes putting another bullet into those they passed. Until they reached her truck.

Luna only thought she was terrified before. Now, she trembled all over. Sweat now ran in rivulets down her face and neck to her chest, wetting the tank top she wore.

This was it. This was how she died. As she reflected on her choice to be here, she didn't know if it was worth it. Sure, she'd saved Markus's life -- for now -- but at the expense of her own. If she knew he'd learn from this and her sacrifice wouldn't be in vain, she'd say yes, it was definitely worth her life to save her brother's. Luna knew he wouldn't learn, though. He'd be right back in the same shape in a month or two. Maybe sooner. So, yes, she was bitter. Not that there was anything to she could do about it now. She'd just accept her fate and hope there was a heaven and that she'd be allowed in.

* * *

Gage Bohannon swept the area for more of the unwelcomed club in Bones territory. The local club had gotten hit first, but Bones had finished all of them. By his reckoning, any club selling drugs in their territory deserved whatever they got. Bones was many things, but they weren't drug dealers, pimps, or a distributor of firearms. They weren't law-abiding citizens -- as evidenced by the slaughter tonight -- but they weren't scum of the earth either.

"One alive in the truck," Deadeye's voice came through the earpiece connected to his radio. "Female. Her hands are still on the steering wheel, which is why I left her alive. There is a gun in the vehicle with her. Along with the hand holding it. Orders?"

"Hold. If she moves her hands or in any way attempts to get that gun, shoot her."

"Copy." He hated giving Deadeye an order to kill a woman, but he wasn't compromising anyone's safety. They'd started this. They'd finish it.

"Keep your hands on that fucking steering wheel," he bit out. "Don't fucking test me or the sniper on you will kill you before I ever give the order." The girl whimpered and squeezed her eyes shut but otherwise didn't move. "Are you armed?"

She took a deep breath, but didn't let go of the wheel or open her eyes. "There's a gun on the floor around my feet somewhere, but that's it. And it wasn't mine. I think the owner left his hand with the gun."

"Good," he said. "You told the truth about that weapon. Are there any others? Knives? Anything?"

"No, sir." Her voice wavered in her fear. Again, that was good. She understood the danger she was in.

"What club do you represent? You don't have colors of any kind. Are you a member? A chaser? An ole lady?" Bohannon had a funny feeling at the nape of his neck. A prickly sensation he knew never to ignore. He didn't think there was danger or his brothers would have known it. It was the girl. Something about her...

"My brother owes Scars and Bars money for drugs. I'm here in his stead. My service for his life."

"You didn't answer my question."

"I'm not with them in any way, nor do I want to be. I just want to get out of this alive so I can tell my brother to go to hell." Fear was making her brave. It surprised Bohannon how much he liked that. It made him want to smile when the circumstances didn't exactly call for it.

"Keep your hands on the wheel until I open the door. I want you to step out. Keep your hands up and open. Keep it slow. Do you understand?"

"I'm scared, not stupid," she snapped, then immediately winced. "Sorry."

Bohannon opened the door to the truck, his gun firmly aimed at her head. If she so much as twitched, he'd kill her himself, saving Deadeye the grief. The girl moved carefully, as he'd instructed. Deliberately. She knew she was in danger. Knew not to fuck with them. That knowledge would make life easier on all of them. The overhead light on the old Ford was long out so there wasn't much of her features he could see.

She uncurled her fingers from the steering wheel slowly, keeping her hands open and at the same level. One leg slid out to place her foot on the ground. Then the other. All the while she never once looked at him. Fear was etched in every move she made. Sweat ran down her arms in streams as if she'd just stepped from a shower.

Once outside, she stood still, hands still in front of her, fingers splayed wide. Bohannon shut the door with a sharp shove of his hand.

"Turn around. Hands on the truck."

She did as told, not hesitating in the least. Her willingness to comply with orders surprised Bohannon. Most mules were just as stubborn as their namesakes. This one seemed more resigned than anything else. She acted as if she had nothing to hide. Maybe she didn't. Or, more likely, she hoped to use her wiles to get herself out of a jam.

As he carefully patted her down for weapons, Bohannon couldn't help but notice her as a woman. She was slight in stature; barely over five feet and svelte of frame. He tried to be as non-personal as possible, but it was difficult when the swell of her breast was just above his palm as he checked her belly for weapons against her skin. His hands were big, and she was so tiny his palm nearly spanned her from side to side yet the curve of her ass was fleshy and rounded, made to tempt a man.

But he was Gage Bohannon. His club name had been Slayer before his brothers sought to mellow him after that stupid TV show became popular, calling him by his last name because the lead character's name was the same. He might enjoy women, might be tempted to do wicked things with the forbidden female from time to time, but he was always in complete control of himself. Now was no exception. She was tempting, true enough. But he had a job to do.

Except his cock had other ideas. Bohannon swore to himself, easily envisioning grinding his hardening erection against that savory ass. He could tell she was affected by his nearness. Either she wasn't adept at staying in control or, more likely, she thought to tempt him with sex. If she did, he'd oblige her. Then take her to his president anyway.

"What are you going to do with me?" Her voice shook, her fear obvious, yet she stayed put, not turning or looking over her shoulder.

"Take you back to our president. We'll discuss the events of the evening then decide what to do next." Not that he needed to give her an explanation.

"Will you kill me?"

"Only if Cain orders it."

She whimpered, her body trembling beneath his touch. She was truly scared, not trying to garner his attention. She hadn't offered herself. Hadn't made an overt move of aggression or seduction. So what was her game?

"What can I do to stay alive?"

Bohannon thought about that. What could she do? "Depends on what Cain decides. If you're looking to convince someone of your innocence, it will be him. I warn you, though, he never goes easy on clubs doing business in our territory without permission. Anything he does to you will be to send a message to Scars and Bars."

"I don't mean anything to them. If he wants leverage on Scars and Bars he won't get it with me. I'm only here to protect my brother."

"Your fate is in Cain's hands," he said. "Accept it. And whatever you do, tell the truth. If you lie, he'll know. You won't get a second chance."

She turned to look at him then. Just a movement of her head, her long midnight hair falling over the other shoulder. When those intensely dark eyes met his, glittering like onyx in the moonlight, Bohannon nearly doubled over as a punch of lust hit him low and mean. He couldn't see her clearly, but there was something disturbing and familiar about her.

"You have to understand, I have nothing to do with the club. My brother owes them drug money. They used me to pay his debt by hauling their... product here."

Bohannon fought off his instinct, which was to comfort and protect her. If ever a female needed protection it was this one. Such a small woman in the middle of a biker war? She was doomed from the beginning. Ruthlessly, he took her wrists and zip-tied them behind her back. "Answer any question Cain asks you truthfully and completely. That's the best advice I can give you."

"And if he doesn't ask me anything? If he's already decided?" Her eyes swam with unshed tears. Her skin glistened with sweat.

"Then he already has the answers he needs. I'll tell him you cooperated in every way with us, assuming you continue to do so. If he decides you need to die, I can promise you'll never know it's coming, and it will be a clean, quick death."

A little sob escaped before she could press her lips together tightly. She ducked her head, breaking her entrancing stare, but not before she got under Bohannon's skin. Why did he feel like he knew her? Lord knew he'd never forget a woman like her, so he couldn't have met her.

Everyone called him Bohannon, but his jacket proclaimed him Slayer because, of all his biker brothers, he had the most kills. He was the enforcer of the club. If something needed doing, he was the one who did it. That way, if the police caught him, they could trace nothing back to anyone else in the club. He'd take full responsibility and shift blame away from his brothers. The name had fit him more than any other, so he thought. This girl, however tested his belief in his job. Could he kill her if Cain ordered it?

"Promise me that if Cain orders you to kill me, you'll at least look into helping my brother."

"Can't do that."

"His name is Markus Newton. He's not a bad man, just... self-absorbed."

Bohannon lost his breath. Before he could stop himself, he snatched a penlight from his utility belt and shone it in the girl's face. *Markus Newton!* A name from his past. Now here was a woman from his past. It had to be. But Markus was more than ten years this girl's senior! Her *older* brother! That son of a bitch should be protecting her, not the other way around.

"Luna?" Her head snapped up, eyes squinting at the bright light. "Son of a bitch." She tried to see past the light but, of course, she couldn't. "Luna Martin?"

"Who are you?" Her voice wavered, even more uneasy than before.

"Are you shittin' me? What the fuck are you doing trying to protect Markus? He's my age!"

She was still for several seconds. "G-Gage?"

"Answer the fucking question, Luna! What the fuck are you doing protecting Markus?"

"He's my brother."

This was insane! Luna couldn't be mixed up in a club like Scars and Bars. Inhaling for calm, Bohannon took a step back from her. Data would have everything on them by the time they got to the clubhouse. He'd know how innocent she was by then.

"Let's go, Luna." God, he didn't need this! Not Luna. Not *his* Luna.

As the headlights of the chaser truck fell over her form, Bohannon shuddered. She shocked him with her striking beauty. She'd always been an exotic little pixy, but this was too much for any man to handle without warning. All that black hair of hers was like a heavy curtain hanging down her back past her ass. Straight. Shiny. Thick. Nearly blue as the light played over it with her movements. Her skin was a delicate earthen tone, announcing her Native heritage. The straight line of her nose was aristocratic and delicate, as were her high cheekbones. But it was those almond-shaped eyes in that intense black that got him. Had always got him. It was as if they bored a darkly hot fire through his heart. With the woman she'd become now, that jolt went straight to his groin. They were guileless. Innocent. He knew from one look she was telling the truth. It wasn't anything she did specifically; it was just there in those onyx depths. No way was she that good of an actor. She hadn't balked at his instructions. Hadn't offered him anything in return for her freedom. Wasn't trying to seduce him. Even once she found out who he was, she hadn't tried to use that to influence him.

She might not be setting out to seduce him -- probably saw him as an old man, a former friend of her brother. But she was doing a damned good job of it anyway.

Once he had her in the passenger side of the chase vehicle Trucker drove, he gave her one last look. "Let's get this over with. Just tell the truth." He glanced at Trucker, who nodded once before putting the cage in gear and starting off. They'd bugged the vehicle, so if she tried to engage Trucker in conversation Data would know. He'd also use any information he got to find out more about her and her brother and their affiliation with Scars and Bars. He hoped she was telling the truth. Because he would make good on his promise to give her a swift, painless death. At least that's what he told himself. He might not be able to bring himself to do the deed if Cain required it. For the first time since meeting Cain and the rest of Bones, he wasn't sure he could live up to the name "Slayer."

Chapter Two

Luna had never been so terrified in her life. She sat in the truck beside the Bones member and waited for her fate. He took her deep into the woods, off the beaten path to what she could only describe as a compound. Or a resort.

Not that it was incredibly fancy, but it was very nice on the outside with carefully mowed lawns and a decent-sized vegetable garden on one side. All illuminated by floodlights spilling over the grounds. A chain-link fence surrounded the property but looked in no way menacing. How that worked she had no idea. Instead, the place gave off an air of security and protection. At least it did until they pulled around back and met three more Bones members.

"Stay here," the driver -- Trucker -- said. Gladly. The last thing Luna wanted to do was get out of that vehicle. If she were going to her doom, she'd rather do it later than sooner.

Gage Bohannon...

How had the one person she needed to find been the man to find her? If anyone could make this right, it was Gage. If he chose to. She remembered the last time she'd seen him. He'd pretty much told Markus to go to hell. Then he'd walked out of their lives. He'd been Markus's best friend. His only friend. And he'd just left. More importantly, he'd left her. True, she'd only been eight years old but he was still her best friend, too. He hadn't looked back. Luna knew because she'd watched him walk away. The one-lane gravel road had been long and straight. She'd watched him until he was out of sight. Not once had he looked back. That night, Luna had cried herself to sleep.

In the parking lot of the compound, the bikers talked. One tall man listened intently with crossed arms, looking deceptively lazy. Everyone seemed to defer to him, to report to him alone as if no one else's opinion mattered. He had to be the Bones president, Cain. Anyone who lived in Somerset, Kentucky knew who Cain was. Most knew him only as a community benefactor though he made no secret about his MC ties. Bones routinely aided the town and specific citizens in dire need. They showed up to every Habitat for Humanity project and protected massive events like Somernites Cruise. All on the down low because more prominent members of the community only saw the biker persona, refusing to give them any credit publicly.

"Bring her to the interrogation room, Bohannon," Cain said, raising his voice. "Once we're done, you can take care of her as you see fit."

That comment sent shivers down her spine. What was about to happen? Her heart pounded with each step Bohannon made toward her. *Bohannon*. Going by his last name suited him better than Gage. The fictional Bohannon couldn't be any more menacing than the real one. The biker.

Once at the truck, he again braced his hands on the open window. "You going to give me trouble?"

Luna wanted to promise him anything just to get him to lower his guard so she could make a break for it, but she could never lie worth a damn. Instead of responding, she ducked her head.

He snorted. "Well, at least you didn't lie." He opened the door. "Come on. Data's already determined your role in this misadventure. I can't promise we'll let you go tonight, but I can promise we ain't gonna hurt you."

Tonight...

He hadn't qualified that promise, but it hung out there like a warning claxon. Luna couldn't help but stiffen when he took her upper arm and pulled her out of the truck. He surprised her by cutting the zip tie free from her wrists. When she looked up at him, he smirked.

"You ain't gettin' away from me, darlin'. Get the thought out of your pretty little head."

Luna bit back a bitter retort, knowing any show of defiance on her part couldn't help. Instead, she let him lead her inside the compound. Again, she was surprised at how nice the place was. Definitely not like the Scars and Bars clubhouse. The inside was neat, clean, and comfortable-looking with plush chairs and sofas in various areas of the great room. The place reminded her of a hotel lobby, maybe? Just not as fancy. It was homey. Comfortable.

They didn't stop there, though. Instead, Bohannon led her through the great room down a flight of stairs to another large room. A wooden stool sat in the middle, a large mat underneath it. Immediately, she had the image of her brother sitting in a similar room. They had used the mat to collect blood as they tortured the person sitting on the stool. Namely, her brother. Was that to be her fate as well? She shivered, not believing Bohannon in the least that they wouldn't hurt her.

She took an involuntary step backward before she caught herself. No. She was no coward. If this was her fate, she'd take it and not make a fucking sound. Chin up, she allowed Bohannon to lead her to the stool and took her seat.

"No matter what you do to me, I can take it," she whispered. Defiant even though she knew it wasn't a good idea. "You won't make me cry."

"Had no intention of it," Cain said as he took his own seat at a semi-circular table. He sat in the center with the Bones officers flanking him on each side. "This is Torpedo, the vice president of Bones," he indicated a man sitting to his right. "You already know Bohannon, our enforcer." The table curved so she was in the center and they could see her from all angles. "I'm Cain. President of Bones. I just have a few questions about your brother. You should know that I already know some of the events leading up to tonight so be careful if you choose to lie." He let those words sink in before continuing. "Is he working for the Scars and Bars?"

"I honestly don't know. All I know is he owes them money for drugs. Whether it was stuff he should have sold but stole, or if he scammed them to get his fix, I don't know."

"I understand why you got involved in this. What I don't know is how. Tell me." Cain spoke matter-of-factly, not in the least abrasive or angry. Just a man listening to her side of the story.

"My brother came to me a couple of weeks ago. Told me he was in trouble again. I told him I couldn't help him. He said they'd kill him if he couldn't pay, but I honestly had nothing more to give him. I would have if I did." She took a breath, rushing through the rest of it. "Anyway, one of the Scars and Bars grabbed me outside my apartment and took me to a room much like this one. My brother was sitting on a chair, though he was in bad shape. They'd beat him. Cut him. Blood was everywhere so I know that mat beneath this stool is to keep from ruining the floor."

Cain shrugged. "And to keep it from soaking into the wood where DNA could be gathered." This was all no big deal to them. She shivered, looking down at her hands. She got the feeling the Bones president said that on purpose just to remind her she wasn't in friendly territory. Luna could have told them she didn't need the reminder. She was all too aware of her situation. Of all the ways she could have met Gage again, this was the worst possible scenario. Not only was she on the wrong side, but he was, quite possibly, a straight-up killer. With her in his sights. "What was their proposition?"

"They wanted me to ferry some... 'packages,' they called them, to the place where you found us. They didn't say why they wanted me for that task or what was in the packages, but I figured the contents had to be drugs."

"Did they tell you they were sending you into Bones territory?"

"No. But no matter where they were sending me, I had to do it to keep my brother alive. When they said they would kill him, I believed them. Besides, I honestly wouldn't have known what it meant if they had told me."

"Data found nothing on you being with any club. Are you familiar with the club lifestyle? Do you know what it means to cross into another club's territory to do business without permission while representing another club?"

"I imagine it's pretty bad," she answered softly. There hadn't been a real feeling of security up to this point, but she was now acutely aware that Cain was the president of Bones.

"If you were a male member of another club, it would be grounds for a beating at best." Cain's expression was blank. He gave nothing away of what he had planned for her. "However, Data assures me you have no ties to Scars and Bars, or any other club, other than through your brother." The Bones president stared at her for long moments before finally asking. "Why didn't you go to the police?"

"You honestly think that was an option if I wanted to see Markus alive?" She didn't mean to sound so snippy, but it wasn't a viable alternative, and they all knew it.

Cain gave her a small smile. "No. I just needed to know if *you* knew that."

"As I told Mr. Bohannon over there before, I'm scared. Not stupid." Luna thought calling him by his last name would distance herself from him. One look, and she knew it made no difference to her whatsoever. He was still her Gage. The man she'd always thought of as hers, even before she knew what sex was. He was just... hers.

Chuckles from a few of the members before they cleared throats or covered mouths with their hand. Even Cain's smile broadened. "You sure you don't belong to a man in a club somewhere? Bohannon! Did you kidnap someone's woman? You have the temperament of an ole lady."

Less than amused, Luna looked him dead in the eyes. "No. And I never want to be."

Bohannon shifted in his seat, drawing her attention to him. Those intense, dark eyes of his met hers with a look so primal she shivered. Everyone else seemed oblivious, discussing her brother and Scars and Bars and how best to deal with both. She and Gage -- no, Bohannon -- however, waged a contest of wills. Luna didn't understand what it was about, but she didn't dare look away. A signaled surrender might cost her more than her brother's debt.

"You realize the Scars and Bars will look for you." Cain addressed her again. It was the only reason she could pull herself from Bohannon's stare.

"I... what?"

"Scars and Bars," Cain said, drawing her back into the conversation. "They'll be looking for you. We destroyed their product so they will want someone to blame."

"Oh, God." The bottom dropped out of Luna's world. She actually saw stars. Her brother could even now be meeting a gruesome end. "My brother!"

"Worry about yourself," Bohannon snapped. "He made his own bed. You don't mule for *any* drug dealer, use up a quarter of the fuckin' load, and expect to get off scot free."

"I know that!" She was feeling desperate. "But he's my brother! I did all this to save his life! Now you're telling me you destroyed any hope I had of doing that?"

"Can't promise we can get him out," Cain said. "And you knew the risks you were taking."

"Then I need to get scarce," she said, her heart pounding. "Run."

"No." Bohannon's voice was like a whip cutting through the room. He didn't shout or speak loudly. Just said that one word. The authority behind it carried at least some weight with their president.

"Speak," Cain said, looking at his brother.

"She was using the options she saw available to her. Yes, she made a choice, but it was under duress." He stood from his seat immediately to Cain's left while Torpedo, their vice president, sat to his right. "I'm putting her under my protection until we resolve this."

Cain sat back, a finger against his lips as he absently rubbed the lower one. No one spoke. Luna was afraid to, unsure of exactly what was happening but knowing her future depended on the next few moments.

"You'll take responsibility for her? Total and complete responsibility?" Cain's gaze never wavered from Bohannon, who met his stare with a steely one of his own.

"I will." Bohannon answered the question without hesitation. "Full disclosure -- I knew her and her brother when we were younger."

Cain turned to Luna. "Do you understand what that means?" She didn't but was still too afraid to actually say so. Instead, she shook her head slightly. "It means that if you betray the club, Bohannon will be responsible for the consequences, both to you and himself. By putting you under his protection, the protection of the enforcer of Bones, he's guaranteeing the rest of the club will protect you. The benefits for you are high... unless you do something foolish. Even to protect your brother."

"You're trusting us to take care of this situation." Bohannon held her captive with his gaze. She couldn't look away, and she desperately wanted to. Looking into the dark depths of his eyes was as mesmerizing as it was terrifying. "I can't promise you we can save your brother, but I promise we'll protect you."

"Sounds familiar," Luna muttered.

Bohannon ignored her. "For now, you'll stick to me like glue. Do you understand?"

"Not really. Seems like I've jumped from the frying pan into the fire."

"Torpedo. Will you help shoulder my responsibilities as enforcer until this is over?"

The man he addressed inclined his head. Torpedo sat on the other side of Cain. The man's dark eyes seemed to take in everything. See everything. All the men interrogating her were scary, but Torpedo seemed worse than the others. Mainly because he was silent. There was no wasted energy when he moved, and anytime he spoke, it was succinct and direct. "Yes," he replied mildly. The gleam in his eyes was anything but mild. The other man looked eager to accept the responsibility.

"I'll defer to you, Cain, but I want this."

For several tense moments, no one spoke. Cain and Bohannon seemed to communicate silently. Both men held each other's gaze in what looked like a battle of wills. Cain's face was as hard as stone. There was something the man didn't like, but Bohannon wasn't backing down. Luna didn't know what to hope for. Seemed like she was fucked either way.

Finally, the tension was too great for her to stay silent. "Do I get a say in this?"

"No," both men said simultaneously. Her interruption seemed to make both men reach a conclusion. Cain nodded once, then stood, leaving the room. All but Bohannon followed him.

"So, am I your prisoner now?"

Bohannon just stared at her. Looking into his eyes was the most terrifying thing Luna had ever experienced. She'd almost rather be back in the woods with a gun pointed at her. This man could hurt her in so many ways...

"I suppose you could look at it that way," he finally acknowledged. "Or you could choose to involve yourself in whatever plan we come up with to free your brother."

"I'm surprised you'd trust me that much."

"I don't." No hesitation.

"Then what do you expect of me?"

"To do what I fucking tell you." He snagged her arm and pulled her along with him. "Come with me."

"Do I have a choice?"

"Not in the least."

Chapter Three

Bohannon didn't take her far. Not even outside the clubhouse compound. The suite he took her to wasn't overly large, but had a separate living and sleeping area. An apartment. The living and dining areas were combined, and the kitchen small, but definitely comfortable for one or two people. She had her own full bathroom as well, and it again struck her at how much like a resort hotel the clubhouse was.

"You'll stay here until I come up with a more permanent solution." Bohannon's tone was gruff, daring her to refuse.

"More permanent? How long will you keep me here?"

"Until you're safe. Do you want to be out in the city, unprotected until Scars and Bars hunt you down? Because, trust me, they're looking for you even now."

Luna gasped. "But it's only been two hours. They probably don't even know something has gone wrong yet."

"They do."

"You seem certain."

He gave her an impatient look as if she should understand everything that had happened. "You don't honestly think we'd deliver a message like that and just leave it to chance they'd figure out who stopped their deal, do you? We dropped every single man killed in that raid on the doorstep of Scars and Bars. The drugs are destroyed."

"Then Markus is as good as dead." Despite the panic welling up inside her and a nearly smothering grief, there was also a humiliating amount of relief. Markus had been in trouble for years. He'd left their parents destitute before they'd passed away, then blown through his part of the life insurance and started working on Luna's. Before she'd realized it, he'd gone through everything she had, and she was taking out loans to bail him out of debts he owed one drug dealer or another. Until this last time, when she'd finally told him she had nothing left to give. Her job in the flooring mill didn't pay much, and she barely had enough for gas to get to work once she'd paid all the loan payments and rent. She practically lived off peanut butter and water as it was.

With relief came shame for feeling that way toward her brother. She didn't want him dead. Quite the opposite. But she wanted the loving person she'd grown up with. Not the drug addict occupying his body. Looking back, his drug use was probably what had driven Gage away.

"We already told you we might not be able to prevent a bad outcome with your brother."

"I know. But he's still my brother." She sighed before sinking into a nearby chair. It wasn't overly expensive looking, but was obviously a quality piece of furniture. What kind of club had she stumbled into? "Look," she said, resigning herself to whatever fate awaited her. "I can't stay here. I have to work. If I miss, I'll get fired, and I can't afford that. Besides the fact I need a place to live, I've got several loans to pay back before I'm truly free of Markus's legacy, no matter what's happened to him."

Bohannon just looked at her.

"I mean, I can't just not pay what I owe."

Still he said nothing.

"I have to work, Bohannon! I have to!" She was getting a little desperate. Though Luna knew he wasn't letting her go, would likely use her part on the earlier misadventure to force her to stay, she had to try.

"You done?"

Fucker. When she didn't respond, he nodded once in a crisp movement. "Good. You'll stay here until we fix this. After that?" He shrugged. "We'll see."

"What do you mean 'we'll see?' You can't keep me here if I don't want to stay!"

Bohannon took the two steps separating him from her and pushed her against the nearby wall. When her hands automatically went to his chest, pushing at him, he snagged both wrists and pinned them above her head in one of his big hands. Luna gasped, her mind telling her she was afraid. Her body told an altogether different story.

It was stupid. He was asserting his dominance over her, not in a sexual context, but in a way to tell her not to go against him. To do as he commanded. Yet, she recognized the dominant lover he would be. His large body so completely dwarfed hers that he could manhandle her and use her body for his pleasure and, as perverse as it was, the thought turned her on more than she'd ever experienced before.

Her breasts ached for his touch. He pinned her between his big frame and the wall and she nearly moaned in delight as his chest mashed against hers. Could he feel her nipples stabbing him? Did she want him to? It was all Luna could manage to not lift her leg to hook around his hip and thrust her pussy at him in invitation.

"No one said you'd stay here against your will," he grated. His voice was husky. Menacing.

Sexy.

Luna couldn't speak. She could be as cutting as the next bitch, but this man was so far out of her league she couldn't form words. He oozed sex and violence, a combination she'd thought she never wanted to experience. Yet, she had the feeling there was nothing this man could do to her she wouldn't enjoy. He was nothing like her. He lived in a world where the rules were vastly different, even though they resided in the middle of civilized society. What startled -- and scared -- her the most was to realize exactly how much she wanted Bohannon in that moment. Despite the situation, despite the circumstances, this was still her Gage. Her mind might scream "no," but her heart screamed a resounding "yes."

When she didn't say anything, simply stood passively beneath him trying to process her own lust, he gave her a humorless grin. The look said he knew exactly what she was struggling with and welcomed it.

"I never keep women who don't want to be kept. But I've been known to make more than one good girl turn rogue."

* * *

The moment her little whimper of need escaped, Bohannon took possession of Luna's mouth. He knew he was being a bastard, but he'd been wanting to kiss her from the moment she'd stepped out of that Goddamned truck. She was too beautiful. Too innocent. If he'd had any decency in him at all, he'd have locked her in his room and left. That wasn't happening. He'd take whatever she wanted to give him and coax a few things she didn't. When it was over, they'd go their separate ways and remember the pleasure they'd shared as a fond memory.

She stood passively for a while, letting him take the lead. Moans and little cries when he nipped her bottom lip sounded like the sweetest music. Bohannon kept her hands pinned in one hand while his other slid the length of her side, molding the side of her breast, her nipped-in waist, to finally settle on the curve of her generous hip. His fingers dug in there, holding her to him.

When she darted her little tongue inside his mouth, meeting his boldly thrusting one with a tentative stroke, Bohannon urged her leg up to circle his hip. He raked his fingernails from the high hem of her shorts down the length of her thigh until he hooked his hand around the back of her knee to keep her where he wanted her.

He pulled back then, needing to see her expression. Hoping to see a dazed look of lust on her lovely face. He wasn't disappointed. She looked stunned and confused, needing more yet unable to express her desires.

Slowly, giving her time to tell him to go to hell if she didn't want more, Bohannon leaned into her, pressing the thickness of his cock to the apex of her thighs. He swore he could feel the heat of her little pussy through their clothing. Instead of rebuffing him, she tilted her pelvis, beginning a slow, sensual movement that ran the length of his dick over and over.

"Little witch." He threw his head back, savoring the feel for that one blistering second. "No," he bit out, leaning his full weight against her so she had to stop moving. "I won't be keeping you against your will." He dipped his head to take her mouth again, thrusting his tongue deep. Holding himself tightly against her, he gave one hard thrust, needing to push her just that much closer to the edge. "But I will be keeping you."

With one last, hard kiss, Bohannon shoved himself away from her. He didn't look back as he opened the door and exited his room. He should really put her in her own room, but he just plain didn't want to. Having her there where he could seduce her at his leisure appealed to him on a primitive level. He doubted Cain would object since he'd pretty much done the same thing to secure his own woman.

Which was why Bohannon needed to confide in Cain his plans for Luna. The problem was he had no clue how far he wanted to take this. Sure, she tasted sweet as fuck and would undoubtedly be even better during sex, but he still didn't have all the information he needed. If she'd been a plant from the Scars and Bars to gain information about Bones, he'd have no choice but to dispose of her. Even now, the thought left a bad taste in his mouth and an ache in his chest. He doubted it was anything so dire as all that, but he still needed the full report from Data before he made up his mind about her.

"You put her in your room." Gavin Ferguson, aka Torpedo, was an ex-SEAL and Bohannon's best friend. Though Bohannon had been a Green Beret instead of a Navy SEAL, the two used their specialized training in a symbiotic way once they'd joined Cain's contracted team of paramilitary in the company ExFil, and had quickly become nearly inseparable.

"Best way to keep an eye on her." Bohannon shrugged as if it was no big deal when both knew it was. The best way to keep a woman from clinging and wanting more than a man wasn't ready or willing to give was to keep them at a distance. And never, *ever*, fuck a woman in his own bed.

"Not buying it," Torpedo said without a moment's hesitation. "You see something in her you want for yourself."

Bohannon tried to sound casual when he replied. "What's not to want? She's beautiful. Seems too innocent to be real. I think I'll enjoy finding out just how innocent she really is."

Immediately, Torpedo scowled, looking for all the world like he might give his brother a beating. "Don't give me that bullshit!" he snapped. "We've known each other too long. Besides, you'd be the first one to say not to treat a woman that way."

"What way? Giving her pleasure she didn't know existed?" Bohannon tried for a cocky smirk but knew his biker brother saw right through him.

"By taking an innocent and shocking her into submission." In all the years Bohannon had known Torpedo, he'd never seen his brother look so angry and disappointed as he did now. "I thought you were better than that, Gage." By calling Bohannon by his given name instead of his road name given by all his brothers, Torpedo made his feelings known.

Bohannon swiped a hand over his face. "I am," he muttered. "I've known her since she was eight and I was twenty-one. I remember the eight-year-old. Not... this. She's... I don't know what she is. But I want her."

"Fine. Wait until this business is over then introduce her to this life slowly. Don't shock her for the sake of your own pleasure. She might enjoy it, but she'll be appalled with herself and never look at you the same way."

"What makes you think I want her to view me as anything other than a badass biker? She's different, but that doesn't mean I intend to actually keep her like Cain did Angel."

"You put her in your Goddamned room, Bohannon! We never do that! Not even with women we're seeing for longer than it takes to fuck them! You want this girl for more than a mere night, and you're fixing to royally fuck up! You know her from your old life? Fine. If you were in that life again, would you be treating her this way?"

That brought Bohannon up short. This wasn't about him mistreating a young woman. This was about Torpedo looking out for Bohannon. Just like he always did. Just like they both did for each other. It was for that reason alone Bohannon could admit the truth.

"I've known this version of Luna a couple of hours. She might be a plant by a rival MC. I should keep my distance, but I can't."

"You're right. You should. You're not going to, so we'll work it out. Now, make sure she understands what's happening and don't treat her like a patch chaser." With that, Torpedo pushed his way past Bohannon and down the stairs to the common room.

Chapter Four

Luna had never been more confused in her life. Bohannon had kissed her with all the finesse of a wrecking ball, made her want him more than she'd ever thought it possible to want a man, then just *left her*. All night. She'd waited for him, knowing he'd be back because, really, who kissed a woman the way he did, mastered her body, then didn't take her? Had he continued his kisses and stroking of her body, Luna knew he was right in that she'd willingly surrender herself to him. Might even *beg* him to take her.

But he hadn't returned. Sometime around daybreak, she'd passed out on the couch, still waiting for him even though that ship had already sailed. Despite how pissed she was, she was equally hurt. How could he force her attention on him in the space of a few hours, then so totally abandon her? More importantly, how could she have let him ensnare her?

She was startled out of a light doze when someone rapped at the door only to open it immediately and stroll in. A woman. Long legs in Daisy Dukes and killer breasts encased in a leather halter. The woman definitely presented her ample breasts to their best advantage as she entered the room. She wore four-inch-heeled ankle boots and let her hips sway in such a way that any man would take a second -- and third -- look. The shock of another woman entering Bohannon's room after the possessive way he'd been with her nearly made Luna see double.

With an exaggerated twist of her ass, the woman walked across the room and looked around, ignoring Luna. After several minutes, the woman finally turned to Luna.

"You'll never stay here, you know," she commented without introduction. "Bohannon never lets a woman stay here. You're not Bones." One elegant shoulder rose, relaying her disdain. "You'll never be one of us."

"No one said I wanted to be one of you." Luna knew she was projecting her fear, anger, and frustration on the woman and the club in general but couldn't help herself. "You're all murderers and gangsters. Every single one of you."

In an instant, the woman lunged for Luna, her red-tipped fingers like claws coming for Luna's face. Luna managed to duck, but took the woman's knee to her midsection, then an awkward slap to her face. Kicking out, Luna knocked her back before scrambling over the couch and running to the table behind her. She grabbed an empty vase. When the woman came at her with a screech, Luna swung. The vase crashed into the woman's head, dropping her. She wasn't unconscious, but dazed.

"Bitch!" the woman screeched

"Me? You're the one who started it!"

"You shouldn't be here! No one wants you here, no matter if you're fucking Bohannon or not!"

"I'm not. And, believe me, no one wants me gone more than me."

"What the fuck is going on in here?" Bohannon's voice boomed from the doorway. His gaze took in the woman on the floor then darted to Luna. She winced at the thunderous expression on his face.

"Your woman here was just inviting me to leave." Luna didn't care if he liked her answer or not, but when he looked even angrier, she took a few involuntary steps backward despite her resolve.

"Inviting her to leave?" His tone was quiet now. Deadly. Now, his gaze focused on the woman hastily getting to her feet, blood streaking down her temple where it had met with the vase. "You unlocked the door to my room while I wasn't here and *invited* my woman to leave?"

"Your... what?" The blonde hussy looked equal parts terrified and baffled.

"Out," he snapped. He didn't mean Luna.

"You can't do this, Bohannon." The woman tried to sound authoritative, as if she had the final say in the matter. "She's not one of us."

Bohannon held Luna's gaze for several seconds. She saw menace. A man in need of violence who would not tolerate being defied. When he slowly turned, the blonde took a defensive step backward before catching herself and raising her chin.

"Jaz, you're not Bones no matter how much you want to be. Don't make me have the patched members remind you of that fact."

Jaz paled but said nothing. She threw Luna a venomous look before hastening out of the room.

For several seconds, Bohannon and Luna stared at each other. Each moment that passed saw Luna getting more and more angry. Finally, she couldn't take the strained silence any longer.

"What." It was an angry demand more than a question.

"She hurt you?"

"What do you care," Luna snapped.

Bohannon closed his eyes, taking a deep breath. When he opened them again, he asked slowly, "Did she hurt you, Luna?"

"No more than I hurt her. I drew blood. She didn't."

"Let me see."

"Like hell! You stay away from me!"

He actually winced but didn't get closer to her. "You know I won't hurt you."

"No. I don't know that in any way!" Now that the adrenaline was leaving her, she started to tremble, her knees going wobbly. She needed to sit down, but that would show weakness. She absolutely refused to look weak in front of this man. Not again. "You're holding me here against my will. You same as told me you're not going to help my brother, but you won't let me go to help him myself! Why would I think you wouldn't hurt me?" The more she spoke, the angrier she got. When she got angry, she tended to cry. "Just let me go!"

As she spoke the last, fury finally overtook Luna. She launched herself at Bohannon, intending to scratch his eyes out. Instead, he caught her by the waist and her hands landed on his broad, strong shoulders. Before she knew it she was pounding Bohannon with fists and open hands, striking hard, nearly hysterically. Luna didn't know why she attacked. One moment she was trembling, swearing to herself she wouldn't show weakness in front of her enemy, the next she'd decided to kill Bohannon. With her bare hands. Not the best of plans, but there it was.

"Hey!" He dodged her blows as best he could, taking the ones he couldn't without retaliation. "Would you stop?"

"Bastard!" She couldn't stop. Would never stop.

"Luna!" Finally, Bohannon had had enough. He carried her the scant few steps to the wall to trap her body between it and his own before securing her hands above her head. "Cut it the fuck out!"

She did, but only because he'd restrained her, taking the fight out of her. Both were breathing hard. Luna was still pissed as hell, embracing her anger so she still got that kick of adrenaline she needed to keep from falling on her face in front of her captor. Or, worse, dissolving into tears.

"Fuck," he whispered. "You're so Goddamned sexy it hurts." She gasped, and he took advantage.

Bohannon's lips met hers, kissing her with something akin to desperation. He took her over, sweeping her into a world of sensation and lust so strong, good sense didn't exist. She was a prisoner. Bohannon's prisoner. Yet she couldn't resist him. In another life, she wouldn't even try to resist him. Some small part of her wanted to seize the fact that he was the Gage she'd adored as a child. The Gage who had adored her. Called her his little Indian princess. She'd love it when he did that. It had made her feel special when her reality was that she was the bastard child of her mother's Cherokee lover. Her father had hated Luna until the day he'd died, despising all she represented. Gage had never made her feel anything but loved and wanted.

Same as he was now.

Bohannon might have started it, but Luna was doing more than merely taking part. When he gave a strong thrust with his tongue, she met it with a thrust of her own. She couldn't stop herself. Something about this man called to something wild and primitive inside of her. For the first time in her life, Luna was equal parts exhilarated and terrified by her own feelings of lust. She couldn't stop. Couldn't pull herself away from him. Didn't *want* to pull away from him. Bohannon had opened up a Pandora's box of sensation she had no hope of closing.

The next thing she knew, he'd let her arms go and she'd wound them around his neck, still kissing him for all she was worth. He walked them to the couch but instead of laying her down and covering her with his big body, he sat so she straddled him. His arms wrapped securely around her, holding her tightly to him. Big, rough palms stroked her back through her tank, snagging on the thin material as he moved.

Finally, one hand settled at the nape of her neck, tangling in her hair, and the other one found her ass, kneading restlessly. His kiss gentled until he finally pulled her head back and trailed his lips and tongue down her neck and back over and over. Luna couldn't help but shiver, little whimpers escaping as he continued to stoke the fire he'd so effortlessly built.

Not long after, he rested his head on her shoulder, his breath nearly as ragged as hers. Bohannon still had his arms tightly around her, but he stopped his brutal seduction.

Luna gasped for breath, her head leaning against the side of his. Her hands gripped his shoulders, and the muscles bunched beneath her fingers. Everything about this man appealed to her other than his lifestyle. How could fate be so cruel to her?

"I'm sorry," he murmured, still nuzzling her shoulder. "I'm supposed to be being good."

She stiffened, pulling back from him. "You... what?"

His hands slid up and down her sides, not allowing her to fully slip away from him, but not restraining her either. Exactly.

He sighed heavily before resting his hands on her hips. "I'm supposed to be taking this slowly. Allowing you to adjust and introducing you to my world a little at a time."

There was something about the way he looked at her and the way he spoke that put Luna on edge. It wasn't that she was afraid of him, per se. She was, but not because of the way he kissed her. Touched her. When he was doing either, she could forget he rode with killers. Was, in fact, a killer himself. "I don't understand."

"I don't either," he muttered. He met her gaze for several moments, searching for something. When she didn't turn away, simply looked at him in confusion, he pulled her back into his arms. "You're too innocent for the likes of me." His voice was a mere whisper. "Way too Goddamned innocent."

"It's not going to matter though. Is it?" Strangely, Luna wasn't scared. Not about this, at least. Why, she didn't understand. Luna wasn't as experienced as some of her friends, but she knew when a man was staking a claim. Right now, Bohannon was claiming her. This was for her. Later would be for his brothers. And she knew without a shadow of a doubt it would happen for his brothers. He'd let them all know she was his. How long he intended for her to be his was something she'd have to figure out, and fast.

"No." He held her gaze. There was hunger there. Raw desire he seemed to want her to see.

"What if I don't want this?" Luna had to ask. Somehow, she already knew the answer, but she needed to hear it from him.

"We'll work through it."

"We? What makes you think I'd even want to work through it?"

"You don't kiss a man the way you just did and not want something more."

"I can't imagine you kissing a woman any differently than you kiss me. I doubt you want to keep every woman you hook up with." Then she blinked, a thought occurring to her. "Or do you? That is what you mean, isn't it? A long-term relationship? An exclusive sexual relationship? Just sex but more than once?" Luna tried to get off his lap, but he was having none of it. "Let me up."

"Stop squirming."

God, he was so… commanding! Luna had never responded to bossy men before, but this one… Bohannon was sin and heaven all in one. She'd only been with one man, but her experience with this one so far was not even in the same league. Probably because he was a *man*. Experienced in all things sexual. What badass biker wasn't? The only thing that truly puzzled her was why she didn't get that oily, sick feeling around him like she had with the men she'd met from Scars and Bars. She hadn't been remotely attracted to any of them. Bohannon was just as big a killer, just as bad a person as anyone from Scars and Bars yet she knew there'd never come a time when she wouldn't be susceptible to his attentions. Maybe it was their past history. Maybe it was the way he touched her. It was addictive and so pleasurable she was putty in his hands.

"There are things I have to take care of, but you're staying with me while I work them out. Then, we'll figure out what to do about you."

"What does that mean?"

"Don't know yet. We'll start with exclusive fuck buddy and work our way out from there."

"Bastard," she hissed, trying even harder to get away from him. Bohannon snaked his arms around her and tightened them. He surprised her by chuckling.

"Goading you is going to be one of the highlights of my day."

"Might get you killed."

He flashed her a crooked grin. "Where would be the fun if getting killed wasn't a possibility?"

God, she was in so much trouble!

Chapter Five

Waking from a sound sleep, Bohannon found his body wrapped around a warm, curvy woman, both of them fully clothed. It took a moment to figure out what the fuck was going on but, once he did, found he was immensely satisfied. Though he hadn't yet fucked her, his little Luna had gotten under his skin in a major way. Surprisingly, it wasn't all sexual. OK, so most of it was sexual. She'd been tentative and reserved -- understandably -- at the beginning. After an hour of just talking to her like a normal person, however, he began to see a highly intelligent, compassionate woman. Very much like the girl he'd known. Everything about her appealed to him. And there was no way she was helping Scars and Bars in any way other than carrying drugs, which they'd forced her to do. Had he met the adult Luna again under different circumstances, he'd already be fucking her.

She hadn't wanted to lie down with him, but he forced the issue. When he'd climbed in behind her and wrapped his arms around her, she'd stiffened, trying to hold herself away from him. Of course, Bohannon was having none of that. He'd simply tugged her closer, resting his chin on her shoulder. After several tense moments, she relaxed by degrees until she was limp. She'd muttered, "This is actually kind of nice," before drifting off.

Fuck. No. She wasn't the type of woman one simply fucked. She was the kind of woman a man wrapped himself up in. Gave her all of himself and was at her mercy. He'd have to think about that later.

Careful not to wake her, Bohannon eased himself from the bed and stood. Blue-black hair spilled around her head like a dark, angelic halo. She was so fucking beautiful it nearly hurt to look at her. Absently, Bohannon rubbed the center of his chest. He'd known the woman Luna for mere hours, and she was already under his skin. He'd wanted her from that first moment he'd seen her clearly, but there was more to her than a pretty face and exotic looks. Hell, he couldn't even damn her brother for putting her in this situation by virtue of the fact it had brought her to him.

As he watched, she turned over, her hand going to the still-warm place on the mattress he'd vacated. When her palm met empty sheets, her eyes fluttered open.

"Gage?" God, that voice. She was drowsy. Sexy as hell. Bohannon could easily imagine he was leaving her bed after a night of passionate, deeply fulfilling sex. She gave him a little frown before he could reply. "I think Bohannon suits you better now."

"Go back to sleep, baby. I have business with my brothers, but I'll be back." At least she understood the changes in him. Neither of them was the same as they were thirteen years ago.

She blinked up at him, still sleepy, but focusing fully on him now. "Is it my brother?"

The sadness on her face nearly broke his heart. "Not going to lie. Part of it is your brother. But I promise I'll do my best to get him out of this alive."

Resignation dimmed those chocolate eyes. "Try. You don't expect to succeed." None of that was a question. Luna was intelligent enough to know the score. Getting her brother out of this mess -- one of his own making -- was going to take a miracle.

"Try," he confirmed. "But I swear to you it will be an honest effort."

One slim shoulder lifted in a shrug. "He's not your responsibility. I'll take care of him."

"He's not your responsibility either, you know. He's a grown-ass man."

"He's my brother."

The two of them locked gazes. Bohannon knew his was hard and unyielding. Hers was quietly determined. She would give him trouble he couldn't afford and probably couldn't contain.

"Do I need to lock you in here? Because I will."

Her expression didn't change. "Do what you think you need to do. I'll do the same."

"Fuck." Bohannon swore under his breath as he sat back down on the bed, reaching for her hand. She didn't fight him, but her fingers didn't close around his in welcome. "Listen to me." He wrapped his other hand around her limp one. "Let me handle this. This is what Bones does. We handle bad shit. We'll get you free of Scars and Bars, then see what we can do about your brother."

"Like I said, do what you feel have to."

"You're not ready to take on a club like this, or any club for that matter. I'd thought you'da learned that the first fucking time. It's how you ended up in this mess to begin with."

Her chin jutted stubbornly. "He's my brother."

"*Half*-brother," he interrupted. She clenched her teeth, visibly angry now.

"*Brother*," she repeated slowly. "I'll protect him with my life if necessary."

"Oh, yeah?" Bohannon snapped the question. "Would he do the same for you? Because, given the dangerous position he's put you in, I'm guessing the answer is no. Bastard probably hasn't changed one Goddamned bit."

"Doesn't matter." No hesitation on her part. "If you do something for someone only because you know they'd do something for you, it doesn't mean anything. I'll do whatever I have to because it's the right thing to do. He's my kin. Kin should stick together."

"Goddamn it, Luna!" He dropped her hand and rose, shoving his fingers through his hair in agitation. "That boy's gonna get you killed!"

"It's still my choice. Not yours. Or anyone else's."

"Fine," he said, stomping into his boots. "Good luck with it. Just don't think Bones isn't going to protect you while you're in our territory. Which, by the way, you're smack in the middle of."

She sat up, drawing her knees to her chest and wrapping her arms around them. "I'll be changing that shortly."

"Like I said. Good luck." Bohannon stomped to the door and shut it more forcefully than strictly necessary. She was in his room, so he wouldn't lock the door, but he refused to move her to another room. She belonged right where she was, damn it!

With a snarl, he took out his cell and texted four prospects. One was to stand guard outside his door while the other two were to post up outside either window. The fourth would keep watch from a distance in case she slipped past the others. Luna wasn't going anywhere.

Just as he was putting his phone in his pocket, it chimed. A mass text to the group from Sword. Apparently, Scars and Bars were building a force nearly twenty men strong. Not surprising. They'd hoped to get their shipment back before it was widely known it was gone. Poacher couldn't let the Florida club know a rival club had bested him. With all the drugs destroyed, not only would he lose one of their main sources of income, he'd lose respect. If he did, he'd lose control of Scars and Bars, something someone looking to seize power within the club would pounce on immediately.

He waited until Clutch was in the hallway headed toward his room. Bohannon nodded once, then left to meet with his brothers. Kickstand and Pig would be in position soon after Shadow took up watch from the tower just inside the clubhouse gate. His position should allow him to keep an eye on Luna as well as watch for trouble. Bohannon replied with the information to the mass text so everyone was on the same page. As lead enforcer it was his responsibility to protect the club first. For the first time in his life, he was torn. He couldn't leave Luna to her own devices. If he did, however, she'd likely do something stupid thinking she'd help her brother.

With a vicious curse, he texted Sword. Bohannon had to let the other man know his conflict. He'd put Sword in charge of the current threat, something he knew his brother would understand. By putting Pig and Kickstand outside Luna's window where Shadow had straight line of sight, he had a triple watch on her most likely escape route, but the two younger prospects weren't exactly top-quality guards. They needed those to guard the compound. Nonetheless, they were men who could be used elsewhere if Sword gave the word.

The common room gradually filled with bikers, from fully patched members to prospects and patch chasers. Everyone with Bones. This was something that affected them all. While only the members had a say in how this was handled, Cain had never had a problem with everyone knowing what was happening with regard to the safety of the club. Anyone who disagreed could damned well leave. Amongst the group, Bohannon spied Jaz headed his way.

Fuck. Just what he needed.

"Not now, Jaz," he warned.

"This is because of that woman, isn't it? Just hand her over, Bohannon. We don't need her kind of trouble." Would the woman never stop? A one-time show of his displeasure was usually enough to send anyone running, even the women of the club who could sometimes be overly aggressive. Nature of the beast. The overblown blonde had been trying to land Bohannon for several months now. Apparently, she was determined to press on even in the face of Bohannon's displeasure. She made no secret she considered him hers and intended to be his old lady. Sure, he'd fucked her, but so had more than one other guy in the club. Jaz wandered from one man to another, and that was fine. No one expected anything other than a hot lay with her, and no one had ever shown any interest in anything else. Why she'd latched onto Bohannon was beyond him, and he didn't like it.

He met Jaz's gaze head on, holding her there for several seconds so she could see he meant business. When she put a defensive hand to her throat, he spoke. "You're one wrong word away from being banned, Jaz. Don't test me."

"Bohannon --"

"One. Wrong. Word."

The woman took a step back, hands up in surrender. "All right," she finally said. "You know where to find me when you need me."

He turned away from Jaz, not wanting her to hold on to anything to let her think he might want her now or in the future. Instead of acknowledging her, he stalked off to find Cain and Sword.

"You good?" Sword didn't beat around the bush.

Bohannon shrugged. "As good as I can be. What's the word?"

"Not sure yet. They're definitely coming to us but haven't sent word ahead what they want."

"Surely they don't think we actually kept any drugs we found," Bohannon said. "We make no secret we destroy any shit we confiscate."

Sword shrugged. "I doubt they believe it. In our place, they certainly wouldn't. Any drugs would be either free use for all or a free nickel for the club. Either way, I'm sure they think we'd do one or the other. Besides, by jumping us as soon as possible, they probably don't think we've had time to destroy it."

"Fine." Cain crossed his arms over his chest. "How long do you think before we confront them?"

"I'd say a day. Maybe less." Sword was rarely ever wrong. Bohannon had trained the Marine when the man joined ExFil. He trusted Sword's judgment. "Wouldn't surprise me if they contacted us tonight."

"We ready?"

"Oh, yeah," Sword answered with complete confidence. "Everyone is on alert and in place. They come to us, we'll shove it down their fuckin' throats."

Cain nodded once. "Good. Move the women who ain't good in a fight and kids to the basement. Make sure your woman knows about the tunnel exit, Bohannon. I don't want any misunderstandings." Cain's gaze darted toward Jaz. Figured their president would know there was friction. The man seemed to know everything.

"Noted. Just so you know, she might not be entirely on board with us yet."

"Didn't expect she would be after her experiences with Scars and Bars."

"She's got one foot out the door."

"So, help her put it back in." Cain raised an eyebrow at Bohannon as if to say "Duh!"

He was about to tell Cain to go fuck himself when his phone buzzed. The text message didn't really surprise him. "Looks like she's already making a run for it."

Sword rolled his eyes. "Used your usual delicate touch, I see."

"Don't worry. She ain't gone yet."

"You going after her?" Sword looked equal parts annoyed and amused.

"What do you fuckin' think?" Bohannon hated snapping at his brother but, really, the man was enjoying himself just little too fucking much.

"Yell if you need help. Girl's a looker."

Bohannon flipped him off as he turned to the nearest exit. His little Luna was turning into a real ache in his side. And his cock. If he were strictly honest, he'd been looking forward to chasing her down. He loved the hunt. Lived for it. In this case, though, the fun would come after he caught her.

Chapter Six

"Might as well get your cute little ass back inside, honey." The voice came from somewhere in the shadows. Luna jumped and nearly squealed.

"Who's there?" She tried to sound authoritative but knew she didn't pull it off. Not even close.

A man stepped into the moonlight spilling across the lawn. He was big and heavily armed, a big-ass military-looking rifle slung across his body. "They call me Shadow," he said, grinning at her. "They say it's not for my skin but my ability to disappear into the shadows, but who can tell with this bunch? They're as politically incorrect as they come." He held out a hand to her. Luna took it and he squeezed gently. His hand was dark and his palm work-roughened. When he smiled at her, gleaming white teeth stood out starkly against the color of his skin.

"I'm assuming you're part of Bones."

"I'm a prospect. By spotting our other trouble on the way *and* managing to corral you, I'm hoping I'll have passed my final test to be a fully patched member."

Luna froze. "*Other trouble.* You mean Scars and Bars? They're coming here?"

Shadow gave a little shake of his head. "Afraid so, little lady. Now, since I know you don't want to hurt my chances at being a patched member, I'm sure you won't mind going back inside where it's safe."

"She won't mind at all." Bohannon's voice practically boomed in the night. Luna couldn't suppress her groan of frustration. Of course Bohannon would be out looking for her.

"Or you guys could just let me go. It'd save you a load of trouble and clear your plans for the night.

Think of it. Scars and Bars will leave you alone, and I can take care of my brother."

Bohannon snagged her upper arm. Luna tried to fight him, but he merely swung her around and grabbed her other arm, shaking her before forcing her on her tiptoes to look straight into his eyes. The man was absolutely *livid*. "What do you think would happen to you if I let you walk outside the protection of this property? What do you think Scars and Bars would do to a woman like you, huh?"

When she couldn't formulate a response he continued. "I'll tell you what they'd do. They'd beat you and Markus both. In front of each other. You so he could see the consequences of his actions. Him so you could see what happens when you fail at a task they set you. Then they'd kill him. Either shoot him in the head or slit his throat. *If* they didn't beat him to death. All of it while you watch. You, they'd rape over and over. Every member of that fucking club would have a go at you. Assuming you survived all that, they'd either use you as the club whore or sell you, depending on the damage they did to your face during your... *lesson*."

With each word, Luna could feel the blood draining from her face. She wanted to deny he knew what he was talking about, but she'd seen what they did to Markus with her own eyes. They had, in fact, beaten him in front of her. Just like Bohannon said.

When she opened her mouth to say something, Bohannon cut her off. "As to the part where Scars and Bars leaves us alone, that's not something related to you in the least. *We* were the ones to stop that drug deal. It was in our territory. They didn't have permission to be there. They'd punish you for losing the stash to us, and your brother for whatever sins he committed against them, but they'll be coming after us for killing their men and bringing Black Reign MC down on them. Black Reign will take revenge on Scars and Bars for losing the shipment they were supposed to distribute for Black Reign. The absolute only thing you'd do by leaving this place is getting yourself killed." He held Luna's gaze while he let the moment draw out. "Eventually."

A heavy but gentle hand landed on her shoulder and pulled her away from Bohannon slowly.

"Relax, Slayer." Luna had forgotten Shadow was still there, a witness to everything Bohannon said. "Little lady ain't going nowhere. She's too smart for that."

Bohannon's gaze shifted away from her to the prospect. Luna didn't know what passed between them, but she saw Bohannon give a curt nod before dropping his hard grip on her upper arms. He sighed, scrubbing a hand over his face. "Did I hurt you?"

She shook her head.

"I need to hear you say it, Luna." He wasn't harsh this time, but his tone brooked no argument.

"No. You didn't hurt me."

He extended a hand to her. "I need you to come inside with me. Bones has the whole place guarded, but it's likely Scars and Bars have scouts casing out the place. I'd rather you be inside where it's safe."

"Is it?" She couldn't help the soft question.

"For you? Perfectly. I swear no one will harm you."

"What about you? You're definitely a danger to me."

He glanced at her sharply. "I'd never hurt you, Luna. Never."

"You told me if Cain ordered my death you'd make sure it was quick and painless. That doesn't sound too safe to me."

Bohannon sighed and pulled her to him roughly. His arms went around her, nearly swallowing her much smaller form. In that moment, Luna felt safer than she'd ever been in her life. Especially since Markus had gotten her involved in his problems. There was no logic to it. Bohannon was quite possibly the most dangerous man she'd ever met. He wasn't the same boy she'd known when she was a child. Bones was definitely more dangerous than Scars and Bars. Yet, right then, she felt protected as never before. Luna found she craved that feeling of security like a drug. The question remained -- was it an illusion?

"I'm not sure I could follow through with that order if he gave it now."

Luna barely heard him. The top of her head where he buried his face muffled his voice.

Giving her one hard squeeze, he let her go, only to scoop her up in his arms and carry her with long, ground-eating strides back to the clubhouse.

Luna had never been one to lie to herself, but she wanted this fairytale Bohannon had woven around her. He was her dark knight, and she was the fair maiden in the tower. Only this dark knight rode a Harley. Not a horse.

* * *

Possessiveness wasn't an emotion Bohannon had any experience dealing with. No one touched his bike, so no worries there, and he'd never even contemplated wanting a woman of his own. When he'd spelled out in no uncertain terms what Scars and Bars would do to Luna if they got their hands on her, everything came crashing down around him. Luna… was his. *Period*. No one, especially not the fucking Scars and Bars, would ever take her from him. She wasn't leaving, no matter what she might think she wanted. She belonged with him. Always had. Bohannon had had her for twenty-four hours. Hadn't had sex with her. Had made no kind of lasting connection with her. But he knew without a doubt he'd never let her go.

"Where are we going?" Her question was tentative, maybe even a little breathless. She'd wound those slender arms around his neck and snuggled into his shoulder all on her own. That was her staking her own claim, whether or not she realized it.

"To my room." His answer was rough, husky. "Where you belong."

Her slender body shivered against his, and Bohannon's cock stood fully at attention, aching and throbbing with every step he took.

Someone opened the door for him so Bohannon didn't even slow down. None of his brothers paid the least bit of attention as he took Luna through the great room down the hall and up the stairs to his room. He noticed Jaz's narrow gaze but ignored her. Unless the woman changed her attitude fast, she was gone.

As he approached, Clutch opened the door, a look of puzzled surprise and sharp disappointment on his face. The man wasn't ready to be part of Bones yet. Once he started training with the others, he'd learn fast enough. He was young yet. Even though Luna had managed to get past him, Bohannon didn't hold ill will toward the man. He'd chastise him properly, but he knew the man wouldn't make the same mistake twice.

Once inside, he locked the door and went to the window. Though his room was on the second floor, the clubhouse was built against the side of a hill. As a result, they built half the bottom floor into the terrain, leaving part of the second floor accessible to the ground. He poked his head outside. Kickstand and Pig had positioned themselves on either side. Pig smoked a cigarette. Kickstand sat with his back to a nearby tree, dozing.

Bohannon gave a low whistle. Pig dropped his cigarette and swung his gun toward the window. "Stay inside, bitch." His snarl made Bohannon want to smack the little motherfucker. "I'll mess up that pretty face of yours if you don't." Kickstand hadn't moved. Neither man would ever make more than a prospect. They were prospects only because they were relatives of Arkham, a patched member but a recluse. The man had wanted to instill discipline into his young cousins and to keep them out of trouble. It wasn't working out as well as they'd hoped.

The plan had been to send the screw-ups back to Arkham, but that threat to Luna was more than Bohannon would tolerate. He climbed out of the window, making as much noise as he could, just hoping the little pissant would make a move on him. Sure enough, Pig stalked toward who he thought was Luna. "I told you to stay the fuck inside!"

Without a warning of any kind, Bohannon stalked toward the boy and, just as it dawned on Pig he was dealing with someone other than a scared female, he backhanded the kid so hard he spun around, knocking into the tree Kickstand sat under. He hit hard enough he bounced off the tree and on to the ground.

"You're too fucking late, boy," Bohannon snapped. "We'll have a discussion about how you talk to women later. Get your cousin there and head to the main house. Tell Arkham what just happened and how

I found you. You don't tell him the whole truth, they'll be consequences."

Kickstand was awake now, on his feet and looking fearful. Pig rubbed his cheek but rolled his eyes. "You didn't have to hit me, bro --" To which Bohannon backhanded him again. It was time to teach those two boys a lesson. Especially Pig.

"Stop it!"

"You don't tell Arkham everything, and the consequences will be a beating like you've never had in your life. Might have done you good if Arkham had beat you long before bringing you here, you little punk. Now get the fuck on!"

He didn't wait to see if the boys did as he told them, merely climbed back inside. Once he'd secured the window, Bohannon leaned his head against the cool glass, trying to get his temper under control. How the fuck was he going to fix this? How to get her to understand?

He turned around to find her standing right where he'd left her, arms wrapped around herself protectively while she stared at him wide eyed.

"We need to talk," he said by way of starting.

"Never had a good conversation start that way, but you're right."

The grin that came to his lips was genuine. Even in the face of a man like him, Luna was brave. A good trait for his woman.

"Everything I've done with you, I've done wrong," he began. "I've deliberately shocked and terrified you, and I don't know how to stop."

"Why?" Her question was asked softly, a hurt and puzzled look on her face. "If I've offended you --"

"No, Luna. It's not your fault. *None* of this is your fault." He scrubbed a hand over his face and crossed the distance to her. Gently, he cupped her face. "There's something about you that's... affected me. I'm not going to sugarcoat this, because I will fuck it up no matter what I do." He closed his eyes and took a breath. "I want you." Her breath left her in a little gasp, her lips parting as if in invitation. It was all Bohannon could do not to groan. "Yes, it's about sex, but it's more than that. I'm a pretty solitary man. My brothers in Bones are the only people who've mattered to me since I left."

"Since you left Markus?" Her voice was small. Thin. Like she was trying to hold back tears, her throat tight.

"No." If he was going to confess he might as well go big. "Since I left *you*."

She jerked back as if he'd struck her. "But you hardly noticed me. I was more of an aggravation than anything. Markus told me so! I was the main reason you left!"

Bohannon ground his teeth. "That little punk is an ass. As far as I'm concerned, he deserves whatever he's getting from Scars and Bars. You, on the other hand, are only in this mess because you have a kind heart. Loving your brother isn't wrong, and it certainly doesn't mean you take whatever happens because you're trying to help him. No matter what the fucking bastard told you, Luna, the choices he made were the reason I left. Not you." He reached out a hand to her, hoping she'd take it. When she just stared at it, he continued. "Don't you remember all the times I let you paint my fingernails pink when we had tea parties while your parents were out late and I stayed to help Markus babysit? I didn't want to leave you with Markus so I even played Barbie dolls with you, for crying out loud!"

Luna was trembling visibly now. Her eyes were shiny with unshed tears. Her lashes spiked with the moisture. "So, I didn't run you off? You didn't mind me always hanging around you?"

"No, baby. You were eight. I was twenty-one. You were like the little sister I never had, and I hated leaving. But I couldn't continue to be around Markus, and your mom, at least, was looking out for you. She knew how Markus was and what he was into. We talked about it at length before I left for the Army."

"I overheard Mom talking with my step-dad. Talking about you going to the military. It had worried them no one could keep Markus out of trouble -- Lord knew they couldn't -- but knew you had to look out for yourself. They also hoped he'd follow you, but he wouldn't even entertain it. I was so upset I confronted Markus."

Finally, she took his hand and let him pull her to him. Wrapping her small body in his arms to hold her solidly against his chest was the best feeling in the world to Bohannon. This was where she was supposed to be. But he was just bastard enough to admit it wasn't all about comforting her. The feel of her lithe form was *maddening*. She likely was only thinking about her childhood where she had no feelings for him other than what an adoring sister might have for a much older brother. He was thinking as a man with a beautiful, desirable woman in his arms. One who could make him lose his mind with just a kiss.

"Is that when he told you it was your fault I left?"

She nodded. "It devastated me, Gage."

"No." He stiffened, pushing her away to force her to look into his eyes. "Gage is the man you knew. The one you thought of as a brother. I'm Bohannon.

You already know the difference, because it's what you call me now when you're not thinking about it."

"I know." She reached up and brushed a lock of hair out of his eyes, her palm sliding down to his beard-roughened face. "So much is different. Your eyes are the same, though. You look at everyone else with a hardness I don't recognize. Me, you still have a soft look for. It's why I've not run screaming yet."

He couldn't help the chuckle. "You did so run. Shadow caught you and let me haul your pretty little ass back here."

"True. But I wasn't screaming."

They shared a soft laugh. Bohannon pulled her to him and kissed her gently before resting his forehead against hers. "I can't... *not* have you, Luna. Not after getting a taste of you."

She stiffened, ducking her head. "You were honest with me so I'll return the courtesy." Bohannon's heart sank. This all had to be too much for her, and he was asking more. Couple that with the fact he was thirteen years her senior, and he could see why she'd be adverse.

"If I made you uncomfortable," he started, clearing his throat, "I'm sorry. I wouldn't have gone as far as I did if you'd given me a sign you didn't want --"

She cut him off with a kiss, licking at his lips until he took over. Bohannon took his time, kissing her thoroughly. If this was the last time he kissed her, he wanted both of them never to forget it. Instead of pulling away from him, however, she wrapped her arms around his neck and continued to kiss him. Everything possessive and male rose up in Bohannon. Her mind might be reluctant, but her body was not. Bohannon knew he could overcome whatever her reservations were.

With difficulty, he ended the kiss gently, not wanting to stop but unwilling to go any further until they were clear as to exactly what he wanted from her. Cupping her face in his big hands, Bohannon stared into her eyes for long moments. Then he groaned and pulled her into his arms, encircling her tightly in a wall of protection he dared anyone to try and break.

Chapter Seven

"Bohannon," she sighed, trying out the name in an affectionate manner. He was right. This wasn't the same man she'd known as a little girl.

"Now, tell me what your objections are."

"I want you, too," she said. "I just don't understand this world. And it's not just the violence. I expected that after seeing what Markus was into with Scars and Bars."

"Then what?"

She swallowed. This was difficult. Not to mention embarrassing. Finally she just lifted her chin and blurted it out as defiantly as she could. "That blonde. My tits ain't that big, Bohannon, and I ain't wearing anything like she did in front of anyone. Not for you or anyone else."

Bohannon's instant and boisterous laughter was at once annoying and hurt just a little. If he was making fun of her, she'd never forgive him.

"It's not that funny," she grumbled, pushing away from him. When he simply tightened his hold on her, that infuriating laughter still making his chest rumble and her nipples tighten, she slapped at him. "Let me up, you ape!" She'd used to call him that when she was really annoyed and it just slipped out.

"Not a chance, my beautiful little Indian princess." His pet name for her when he was trying to rile her. When she was eight, it had made her kick him in the shins more than once. Now, it softened her heart, any resolve she might have held on to flying out the window. "We talk this out now so I can fuck you later."

She exhaled in a rush of white-hot heat. He'd murmured his wickedness next to her ear so his breath tickled, causing more sensation. "What makes you think I'm going to let you? I'm pretty sure I'm angry with you for laughing at me just now."

He nuzzled her hair out of the way only to tug on her earlobe with his teeth. "I wasn't laughing at you, sweetheart. I was laughing at myself. Because I can just imagine my brothers' reaction when I started killing anyone who even glanced your way if you wore something like Jaz had on. Sure she has big tits, but she's overblown and does it to attract a certain kind of man. You, on the other hand, just scream natural beauty. Any man in this club would love to get your clothes off and appreciate the treasure you are. I'm not at all good with that. If I get my way, I'll have you covered from neck to toes in something very unflattering."

That got Luna to giggle. Just a little. Until she was actually clinging to Bohannon, laughing until tears streamed down her face. "I don't even know what to say to that."

"You say nothing. Just tell me what else is bothering you. What else do I have to make better before you accept you're mine?"

The smile faded from her slowly, and she again raised her hand to his face. His beard was rough, but not prickly. She found she liked the texture and wondered what it would feel like against her skin. That thought made her tremble because she knew that was exactly what he intended to do. He'd use it as a sensual weapon against her. She'd lose her mind and let him do whatever he wanted. "I know Bones doesn't care what happens to Markus, but I do. I have to save him. At least give him a chance to pull his life together."

His expression instantly went blank, and Luna could see this wasn't a laughing matter to him. He took the subject of her brother very seriously. "I won't lie, Luna. Never to you. And never to get what I want from you. I'll do my best to see him helped, but I won't promise. He's a grown-ass man, more than ten years older than you. You shouldn't be the one trying to save his soul, Luna." He held her gaze for several moments before continuing. "As far as I'm concerned, he's already betrayed you by dragging you into his mess simply to save his own ass. When Scars and Bars come for you -- and they will come for you -- if he's with them, he'd better prove he's there to save *your* ass. If not, there's nothing I can do for him."

Luna absorbed that. Took his words in and truly processed them and all they meant. After long moments, she nodded. After all, Bohannon was right. "I love him, Bohannon."

"I know, baby. But he's a man. He's made his own choices and damned the consequences. He has to live with them now."

"What about me? I have to live with them, too."

"No, honey. You're making yourself live with the consequences of his actions because you love him. What you haven't realized yet is that you can't keep making yourself miserable for someone who doesn't appreciate what you're doing and doesn't care that you're miserable. You've tried everything, even to the point of putting yourself in danger. It stops now. It stops because I'm taking over, and you're going to let me. Why? Because I have your best interest at heart." When she opened her mouth to protest, he added, "And because I'm bigger than you. I can -- and will -- force the issue."

Luna gave a little exasperated snort. "I was with you until the end. You just had to go all macho on me."

He grinned. "I'm the enforcer of Bones, my little Indian princess. It's not in my nature to coax, or even ask. I just do what's necessary to safeguard my club. Like it or not, you're part of my world now. You're included in that circle of protection."

"Are you always such a bully?"

"No. I'm usually worse. I'm being semi-civil for you."

His eyes glittered with teasing mirth, but Luna knew he was serious. "But you'll at least give him a chance?"

"For you. No one else could persuade me to do anything other than let nature take its course. For you, I'll give him the choice of his freedom, or becoming a prospect for Bones. Like Pig and Kickstand. It'll allow us to monitor him. He don't walk the straight and narrow, he gets convinced he needs to."

"And if it doesn't work?"

"We'll deal with that if we come to it. Don't borrow trouble, princess."

"That's probably the only chance he has." She looked up at him, again stroking his face. "I can't ask for more than that, Bohannon."

"We good then? Because I have plans for you tonight, and they don't involve your fucking brother in any way."

* * *

The woman would be the death of him, Bohannon decided. Not only did she have him wrapped around her little finger, but she truly didn't realize it. She could ask for the world, and he'd give it to her. Saving her brother seemed a small price to pay. Cain would probably kill him for even considering Markus as a prospect without consulting the president.

As a rule, only serious men were considered as prospective club members. They'd made an exception for Arkham's young cousins because of sacrifices Arkham had made on behalf of the club. Bohannon was pushing and knew it.

"Plans?" Luna swallowed, but nibbled her bottom lip. Bohannon knew women. This one was interested. She just didn't know how to express that interest.

"Oh, yeah. Unless you tell me not to, I'm going to do wicked things to your little body all fucking night."

"What kind of wicked things?"

That was the exact right question. Bohannon took it as his permission. He pulled her closer, lifting her until she wrapped her legs around his waist. "How 'bout I show you?"

Between kisses, she breathed, "Yes. Do that."

The bedroom wasn't nearly close enough, but Bohannon sure as shit wasn't taking her anywhere else for their first time together. Later, after he'd explored every inch of her lush curves, learned what every sigh, cry, and scream meant, he'd take her all over the fucking place.

How he made it to his bed, Bohannon would never know. He certainly bumped into more than a few things. He seemed to remember knocking over a lamp somewhere, but wasn't sure exactly where. By the time he got them into the bedroom and kicked the door shut, he was ravenous for her.

Luna tugged at his clothing the same as he did hers. When he finally had to set her on her feet to tug off his boots, she was shedding clothing just as fast as he was. She was so much smaller than him! Just watching as his hands nearly spanned her tiny waist was a huge turn on. His cock ached like a motherfucker, and he was barely holding himself together.

Her breathing came in quick little pants, whimpers occasionally escaping when she couldn't get undressed fast enough. Those sounds only fueled his own growls of need and the desperate desire to claim her for his own. Luna kept glancing his way, as if to make sure he was still there. Bohannon never took his gaze from hers, needing to make sure she was really doing this because she wanted to. The last thing he wanted was for her to think sex with him was the price for her brother's life.

Finally, when they were both naked, he tossed her on the bed and covered her with his much larger frame. "Look at me, baby." He threaded his fingers through her long silken tresses, forcing her to obey him. "This is us. No one else. Don't do this if it's not exactly what you want. I'm a bastard, but I'm not fucked up enough to make you trade your body for your brother's life."

She blinked up at him, clearly confused. "I... what?"

He cleared his throat, wincing at his bungling of something so fucking important. Unfortunately, his brain had deserted him. He was reduced to nothing more than primal instinct. "Don't fuck me because you think it's the only way to save Markus. Fuck me because you can't stand for me not to be inside your little cunt one more second!" His hand tightened in her hair, forcing her to really see him. He knew he couldn't disguise the need he had. Not only was his cock hard as fucking steel, but there was no doubt in his mind his expression was brutally intense. There was no way she could fail to notice either. And he wasn't altogether sure he could stop himself if she denied him.

"Bohannon, you're the only person in my thoughts right now. So put up or shut up, biker boy."

There was a silence while Bohannon tried to process this. She was a snippy little thing. Which gave him enough control to prevent himself from cramming his dick inside her to get some semblance of relief. Which would have been a terrible idea. He let out a breath and a short, barked laugh came out instead.

"You're priceless," he finally managed between chuckles. "So Goddamned priceless. And you're all mine."

"I am." She stretched languidly before growing serious once more. She laid one small hand on the side of his face, petting his beard as if fascinated with the texture. "I have a confession to make, and now seems like the best time."

Bohannon cocked his head, sensing a trap but not really caring. She'd trapped him from the first second he'd realized who she was. "And?"

"When I was a little girl, I always thought of you as mine. I think that was what hurt most about you leaving." When he opened his mouth to question her, she cut him off with those small fingers to his lips. "I don't mean in a sexual way. That's not even remotely close. I mean, like… I don't know." Her brow furrowed as if she were trying really hard to explain but not certain she could even understand it herself. "I just thought you'd always be in my life. Like we were partners. We'd always be together in a happily-ever-after sort of way."

"We will be, Luna. I swear it."

"Then prove it," she challenged, her eyes glinting in her own mirth. "Make me yours."

"You have to know, once I do this, it's done. Hell, it's already done. You're never leaving me, no matter what."

"You aren't listening to me, Bohannon." She smiled even as she tugged on his beard until she could lick at his bottom lip. "I'm the one not letting you go."

It was all the encouragement he needed. Bohannon clung to Luna like she was his last lifeline. In a way, he supposed she was. Leaving that impossibly sweet eight-year-old had been the hardest thing he'd ever done. Protecting her had always been a priority to him, but he'd been a twenty-one-year-old with no real idea of how the world worked. If he'd stayed, it would have been weird. Leaving and hoping Markus would follow him had been the logical choice. The best choice for him. Had it been the best for Luna?

Right now, her tongue danced with his, forgiving anything he felt the need to ask her for. She wanted him. He wanted her. She wasn't that innocent eight-year-old, but he wasn't the naïve twenty-one-year-old hoping to save a little girl with no real understanding of why he felt that way. They were both adults. If she was too young for him, that was their business. No one else's.

Bohannon pressed his full weight on Luna, loving the way his body covered hers completely. Only her limbs were free, and she wrapped them around him, holding him to her the same way he was trapping her to him. They kissed for long, long moments. Bohannon savored the luxury of simply doing that. But her breasts stabbed into his chest, their nipples like little pebbles trapped between them. Her pussy was wet and growing wetter by the second. Her whimpers escaped with increasing fervor as they kissed, and she rocked her pelvis against his abdomen, leaving a slick, damp trail on his skin.

"God, woman," he bit out hoarsely. "Need you bad!"

"Need you too, Bohannon!"

"Can't do this right. Can't take my time."

"I'm ready for you. You know that." Her voice was a mere thread of sound, the needy timbre tugging at his cock as if she'd reached between them to stroke him.

"You been with a man before?"

She blinked, again, looking adorably confused. "I... yes. One."

A seething rage bubbled up inside Bohannon he needed to suppress at all costs. It wasn't the fact she'd been with another man. He'd been with more women than he could count. Still, he wanted to find the fuck who'd taken his woman's virginity and pound him into the ground.

"He make it good for you?"

"I thought so," she confessed, still arching against him. Her breasts slid up his chest in a sensual glide as her pussy moved over his abdomen. His cock was tucked beneath her ass, occasionally pressing between her cheeks to nestle there. Which wasn't helping anything. "But I've never felt like this. Never."

"Did he at least get you off?"

"Why are you asking this now?" Her question was all but a wail. Luna was beginning to thrash beneath him. One hand went between them to grasp his cock, aiming it where she needed him most. At the first touch of her wet little cunt around the head of his dick, Bohannon nearly shot off. Somehow, he stilled her. He snatched her hand away, pulling both of her arms above her head and holding them there in one of his. His body pinned hers to the bed ruthlessly, not letting her do much more than breathe. Still, she wiggled.

"Because I'm going to make you come so hard and so fucking many times you're mindless with it, and I need to know if you can handle it!"

When she only blinked up at him, her mouth forming a silent "O" of surprise, he let his cock find the cleft of her pussy and rocked against her. He swore he could feel her little clit pulsing against him as he rubbed over it.

"Bohannon, please! I need you inside me!"

"Answer the Goddamned question!"

"No! He didn't make me come! It was good, but I've only ever gotten off by myself!"

A groan of defeat was pulled from Bohannon's chest. The images her confession put into his brain were wicked. Sinful, even! He'd explore every single one of them with her, too. Just not now. Now, he needed to be inside her. To fuck her until they were both eased. He knew he'd never be satisfied. Not with Luna. She could make him a beggar with how much he needed her.

"Fuck," he swore as he guided the head of his cock to her entrance. "Gonna fuck you all fucking night." With that, he eased himself inside her, taking his time to savor the first experience.

She was tight, and so fucking hot he couldn't believe this was actually happening. Luna shuddered against him, digging her heels into his ass and urging him on. When he slid out of her, she cried out, tightening her hold on him until he eased back inside her. Farther this time. Out. Back in. Until, finally, his balls tucked against her and they were joined fully.

"Now, my little Indian princess. We fuck."

"Yes," she breathed. "Oh, God, yes!"

He released her hands as he began a slow, sensual movement, gliding in and out of her in measured thrusts. He held her gaze, needing to make sure he wasn't hurting her before he completely lost his mind.

"You good?"

"No! I'm *dying*! *Move*!"

Had this been a normal encounter, Bohannon would have laughed at the little bite to her voice. Instead, he buried his face in her neck and bit down as he surged into her with ever-increasing thrusts. "Little wench!"

* * *

"God! Bohannon!" Luna planted her feet on the mattress and used all her strength to meet Bohannon thrust for thrust. It didn't take her long to find his rhythm and match it, bringing their bodies together with a steady *slap*. She'd told Bohannon the truth about her previous encounters. They'd been pleasant, but nothing like this. Maybe her choice of lover hadn't been good. He'd been her age, and they'd only had sex twice. Neither of them had much experience, and it was more enthusiastic then skilled. This was... *both*. And intense. She could tell when she looked into his eyes, when she felt his body shuddering above hers, he was just as affected as she was.

Even pleasuring herself, nothing even came close to this. Maybe it was the man. Maybe it was his confident skill and expert touch. All she knew was she was holding him to his promise. He was hers just as she was his.

As he drove in and out of her, Luna's breath came in little gasps. She met him eagerly, needing everything he gave and wanting to reciprocate. She scratched her nails down his back -- which he seemed to revel in -- and slid her hands down to his ass. Taking a firm grip on each cheek, she sank her nails in, digging into him like spurs to a horse.

With a harsh cry, Bohannon shifted to put his weight on one shoulder, never slowing or ceasing his movements. One hand found the delicate column of her throat, and he held her steady. When she tried to rise, intending to sink her teeth into his shoulder, he tightened his grip on her ever so slightly and snarled at her.

"Stay down!"

She bared her teeth at him. Luna had never acted like this in her life. Never *wanted* to. This was raw. Primitive. Two people both loving each other and establishing dominance. While she didn't want control of him, she wanted him to know she was staking a claim on him the same as he was her. "You tell your bimbo that, too? Because I'm not a biddable hussy so enamored with your cock I'll do everything you say."

Luna nearly regretted her outburst until an answering fire lit his eyes as he continued to fuck her. "You'll do what I say, when I say. Right now, you lie still while I fuck you. Don't you fucking move!"

"And if I don't?"

"I'll flip you over, pin your hands behind your back, and fuck the living hell out of you, woman!"

Oh, God! That was all Luna could take. Her cunt spasmed as her orgasm exploded inside her. She screamed her completion and wrapped her legs tightly around him, locking them at the ankles.

"Fucking hell!" Bohannon swore viciously, a string of epithets that would have set her ears burning if she weren't already on fire. "Making me come! Let go if you don't want my cum in you!"

"Not letting go," she bit out between contractions. "You need to come now? You'll do it inside me or not at all!"

"*Fuck!*" That was it. Luna felt him ejaculate inside her, one hot spurt after another. She came again, this time a rolling tide of sensation that went on and on and on.

Finally he collapsed on top of her, still thrusting. His body trembled over her with every slide of his cock, with every squeeze of her pussy around him. They stayed locked together for long, long moments. It was a little hard to breathe, but Luna kept her arms and legs tightly around him, not wanting him to separate.

"Please tell me I didn't hurt you, baby." His softly spoken words were muffled in her neck where he nuzzled, kissed, and licked. "I never want to hurt you, and I was rough."

"You were exactly the way I wanted you," she said, kissing his neck. "I've never had so much pleasure or felt so much love as I did just now."

He pulled back to look at her, not even bothering to deny there had been love in his touch. "Then I did my job."

She smiled. "You did indeed."

"You on the pill? Bit late in the asking, but I want to know."

Luna bit her lip, for the first time feeling the twinge of guilt. "I won't lie to you. I'm not. And if I'm pregnant, I won't regret it. Even if you didn't really mean you wanted me for the long term."

An impatient look followed her words. "Don't be ridiculous. You know I want you long term. And I want you to have my babies. I only asked so I'd know what to expect. If you're pregnant, I'll take care of you and my kid."

"I know you will. Just wanted you to know I wasn't trying to trap you. However, you've got other women hanging around. I'm not much of a fighter, so maybe I should stake my claim the only way I can."

Bohannon snorted. The smile lit up his face like magic. Gone was the scary warrior she'd met in the woods. In his place was the man she'd worshiped as a child. For the first time, Luna was able to reconcile one with the other. They were both Bohannon. The tender man who would let a child paint his fingernails and toenails pink in order to make sure she was safe was also a bold, fierce warrior. One who would kill anyone trying to harm that child he guarded.

It was then Luna realized she was truly in love.

Chapter Eight

"Cain," Sword called as he entered the clubhouse common room. "Poacher is on the way up the drive with a full contingent. They look ready for war."

Cain chuckled. "Bringing it to our door, are they?"

"Looks that way." Sword was the second enforcer of the club. Cain might have been amused, but Sword was not. "You'd think they'd've learned a lesson when Kiss of Death tried the same thing. Bringing their muscle right to our door."

"By all means, give them a warm greeting." Cain pulled his wife, Angel, into his arms and kissed her forehead before bending to give her instructions. Angel was the only person Cain ever showed tender emotion for. It was obvious Angel wanted to be at his side, but Cain simply cut off her protest with a hard kiss, swatted her ass, and sent her out of danger. The young woman blushed, looking around her self-consciously, but did as Cain told her, heading to the basement of the clubhouse.

Bohannon had tried to send Luna to the basement when he realized there'd be trouble. Sword had texted them all about the buildup of Scars and Bars members, and everything in him screamed to force her compliance. He knew she'd be the primary focus of the other club and knew he couldn't protect both her and Cain. She'd looked terrified, but stubbornly refused to hide while he faced this group partially on her behalf.

That had been her excuse, but Bohannon knew the real reason was fucking Markus. She'd looked just as scared as she had when he'd first pulled her from that damned truck a couple of nights ago but she hadn't backed down. Torpedo had been right. Had he continued to scare and shock her, she'd have bolted. Possibly right into the hands of Scars and Bars. Now, he just wanted to kill all these motherfuckers so it would be done. Her brother included. Which was what had led to the fucking problem in the first fucking place. She knew every second he thought about how Markus had put her in so much danger the more murderous he grew.

Unfortunately, he couldn't kill everyone threatening Luna without bringing law enforcement down on them. Well, he could, but it would require the help of the entire club, and he wouldn't put his brothers in that position. This would be a tricky situation. No matter what happened, it wouldn't be over tonight.

All members of Bones in the clubhouse meandered outside, unhurried and unconcerned. What the Scars and Bars wouldn't see were the four snipers on the roof sighting them up for when diplomacy fell by the wayside.

Sixteen Harleys roared up the drive to line up in front of the Bones clubhouse. They revved their engines in a menacing display. What they didn't understand was the noise would never intimidate Bones. Thunder never hurt anyone. Bones was the lightning.

Once Scars and Bars finished with all the blustering, Poacher got off his bike and stalked toward Bones. His enforcers flanked him. All but one had their weapons holstered. His lead enforcer had a pistol gripped in a hand at his side. Normally, Bohannon would keep an eye on the guy, putting himself in the best position to protect Cain. This time, however, he drew his gun as well, chambering a round in the SIG Sauer as he walked. Cain gave him a side eye but said nothing, nor did he wave Bohannon off. The president might not like his actions, but he wouldn't reprimand Bohannon in front of another club.

"Poacher." Cain acknowledged the other president. "Normally I'd pretend I was happy to see another club visiting, but, since your muscle is blatantly sporting loaded guns inside our own fucking clubhouse territory, I'll simply ask what the fuck you're doing here."

"You know why I'm fuckin' here! You've got goods that belong to me, and a fuckin' whore traitor!" Poacher pointed toward the clubhouse, where Bohannon knew Luna stood with several patched members protecting her. Her being outside at all was a sore spot with him, one they'd argued about, but he understood and respected her need to face her problems. Didn't mean he had to like it. She also seemed to accept the man he'd become. He still didn't want her to see him kill. 'Cause one more word, and this motherfucker was a ghost.

"Suppose you enlighten me. What are you referring to? And I caution you to watch your fuckin' mouth."

Poacher took two steps toward Cain. When Cain didn't back down but took a step forward himself, Poacher snarled. "You got my smack, you son of a bitch. And the bitch over there is my mule."

Bohannon could almost admire the man for not backing down. Cain, when challenged, was scary as shit. Like right now. The look in Cain's eyes could make a pussy of the hardest of men. With all his muscle here, however, Poacher couldn't afford to look like a pussy.

Cain shrugged casually, as if it was all no big deal. The way his body looked deceptively relaxed said he was anything but casual. "Smack's gone. The woman belongs with Bones. You want her? You gotta take her." Bohannon glanced at his president, barely able to contain his protest, and saw a smile that was more a baring of teeth. The smile of a killer looking for a fight. "You gotta take her from *all* of us."

"She ain't nothin' to you, Cain," Poacher spat. "But she's *our* mule."

"So? Come get her. Give your life for your club to get her back, you son of a bitch." Cain withdrew his own weapon and cocked it, pointing it directly at Poacher's face. Bohannon grinned, following suit, his weapon leveled at the president as he pulled a second pistol from the small of his back, cocked it, and aimed at the Scars and Bars enforcer.

Every member of Bones followed Cain and Bohannon's example, targeting a member of the rival club. Which prompted the other men to draw their guns. Which prompted one of the snipers from the roof -- probably Deadeye -- to fire a shot at the president's feet, not two inches in front of the man, with a suppressed rifle. There was only a muffled *thump* as gravel and dust puffed up from the ground. No one would be able to tell where the shot came from.

"Fucking bastard!" Poacher was livid, but his muscle seemed to know the trouble they were in and held fire. "I'll fucking kill every Goddamned one of ya!"

Bohannon could tell Poacher wasn't letting this go. No president could. With Bones firing on them, Poacher had to reciprocate. Even if it had happened in Bones territory.

Sure enough, the Scars and Bars president took aim at Cain. Before he could even pull the hammer back, Bohannon and Cain fired simultaneously, taking

Poacher in the head and chest. Both a kill shot. The club president dropped, and all hell broke loose.

Bohannon's next shot was at the enforcer while Sword shoved Cain behind him even as the Bones president fired his Glock twice in quick succession. The other Scars and Bars members fired several times, but Sword and Bohannon dropped two more with another shot each.

For the first time in his military career, Bohannon's attention was divided. He knew Luna was in the line of fire. If one of those fuckers wanted to kill her badly enough for what they perceived as a betrayal, there wasn't much Bohannon could do to protect her. He should have fucking tied her up and locked her in the fucking basement!

Sweat broke out over his skin, and rage threatened to overwhelm him. His heart pounded out a steady rhythm of fear, and the taste was exceedingly bitter. He wanted to find Luna. Make sure she was good. But he didn't dare take his eyes off the enemy. Any of them could be the one trying to take her out. In that moment he knew, no matter how much trouble it caused his brothers, no matter if it meant he spent the rest of his life in prison, if he had to kill every single one of these motherfuckers to keep Luna safe, it was exactly what he would do.

With a battle roar, Bohannon fired repeatedly as he moved forward, winging one man and catching another in the leg. His SIG Sauer boomed with each pull of the trigger. He advanced steadily, stopping only when he felt a hand on his shoulder. Still, Bohannon continued to fire.

"It's over, brother," Cain shouted at him even as he shoved one of Bohannon's arms down, trying to get him to stop firing. He and Sword both pulled

Bohannon back, urging him to lower his other weapon. He heard them as if in a long tunnel, calling him to them when all he wanted to do was kill.

He tracked the remaining men, unable to simply stand down, the bloodlust too close for that. The rest of Scars and Bars had dropped their weapons and taken cover, yelling out their surrender, their hands in the air. The whole thing lasted all of thirty seconds. Sweat stung Bohannon's eyes, his heart still pounding a furious rhythm.

"Luna," he gasped. "Where's Luna!"

As if a light shone down from the heavens above, he saw her hurrying to him with the sunlight gleaming off her shining black hair. The enemy was still at their doorstep. Any of them could make a try for her at any moment. Bohannon could no more have sent her away than he could walk on the moon. Instead, he caught her as she flung herself at him, wrapping his arms tightly around her. He was careful to keep his body between Luna and the Scars and Bars members.

"Sword." Bohannon found the other enforcer's gaze and held it steadily. There was no way he could hide the wildness in his eyes from his brother. Sword would know the desperation he felt to get Luna away from danger and how it warred with the need to clean up the mess on their home turf.

"I've got this. Get her out of here."

As the last word passed Sword's lips, a shot rang out. Luna jerked violently and gave a sharp cry. Warm blood sprayed over Bohannon's face as Luna's body went limp in his arms, a hole blossoming in her upper forehead just before the exiting bullet whizzed directly beside Bohannon's ear.

Chapter Nine

Two months later...

Bohannon woke up screaming and drenched in sweat. His Luna was shot. *In the head!* She lay dying in his arms, and all he could do was roar his anguish. Until he'd beaten the motherfucker to death with his bare hands. It hadn't helped. Luna was still gone.

"Bohannon." A soft, feminine voice beside him called him back to reality.

Luna?

But... wasn't she dead?

"Baby, it's OK. I'm OK. Wake up and look at me."

The bedside lamp clicked on, a soft glow filling his bedroom. Luna was, indeed, beside him. The bandage wrapped around her head like a turban was long gone, and she didn't seem to have had any lasting effects. Every day, Bohannon thanked whatever god had smiled down on him she hadn't been taken from him.

"Are you back with me? Look at me." The command was soft but no less compelling. Bohannon rubbed his eyes, blinking back the tears he knew were tracking down his face and...

She was truly there. Right in front of him.

"Fuck," he whispered brokenly before reaching for her, pulling Luna into his arms to wrap her in a cocoon of protection. "I lost you," he managed, his voice sounding suspiciously like a sob to him. "I fucking *lost* you!"

"No, you didn't. I'm right here. I got lucky."

"No. *I* got lucky. And, Goddamn it, I want to kill that fucking son of a bitch again! I can't say I'm sorry, either. Luna." He looked at her, framing her face with his hands.

Until she reached out with gentle fingers and wiped the moisture continuing to drip beneath his eyes, Bohannon hadn't realized he was still crying. "I killed your brother with my bare hands. Beat him to death right in front of you."

"I was unconscious. And he shot me. I loved him with all my heart, but *he shot me*." She continued to caress his face, wiping tears away with tenderness until she finally leaned forward and simply kissed them away. "I'm OK with what you did. I hate that it had to be you, but I'll never hold it against you. I don't even mourn him as I probably should. You did nothing wrong, baby. Do you hear me? Nothing!"

This wasn't the first time she'd had to do this. To Bohannon's shame, it was near nightly. The shock of the whole event was still close, though he tried hard to block it out, just like any other unpleasant mission. This time, however, the carnage had hit too Goddamn close to home.

The doctor had said she was lucky. The bullet had flown straight and true, entering and exiting the upper portion of her brain cleanly. Had it happened anywhere else, she might have never been Luna again. Assuming she'd even lived. As to Markus, Poacher had told him the only way he would live was to kill Luna. Apparently, Poacher had been convinced Luna had been responsible for the whole mess. Black Reign was breathing down his neck and someone had to be punished. It came down to Markus or Luna. Markus might still be of use to them, but Luna…

Bohannon pulled her into his arms and kissed her like a starving man led to water. When this happened, he needed her. She knew and understood, always welcoming him with her body and her kisses. She never rebuffed him or said or did anything to make him feel like she couldn't get past the death of her brother, but he thought he might always be afraid she would. Luna had to constantly reassure him she was his.

Bohannon thought it made him weak, and maybe it did. Didn't change the fact he still needed it. If she thought him weak, she didn't seem to mind and never said so or gave indication those were her thoughts. Instead, she just smiled and welcomed him with open arms, loving him in that complete and total way she had. The way he'd come to crave.

"Not sure I can be gentle tonight," he said as he slid his hand down the curve of her hip. He took one nipple into his mouth and tugged with his teeth until she gasped and arched, offering himself to her.

"No one said I wanted or needed gentle. Doc says I'm fine. I swear to you I don't feel any pain. Anything still lingering is purely cosmetic. And if you can live with that, so can I."

"As long as you're here with me, I could give two fucks what your forehead looks like. You're here. You're well. *You're mine.*"

Bohannon maneuvered her to the center of the bed on her back, spreading her legs and pinning her knees beside her so that she lay open and completely exposed to his hungry gaze and mouth. He wanted to look his fill at the small strip of hair pointing straight to heaven. She kept the rest bare, and he loved the way it felt against his tongue. Moisture glistened between the delicate folds of her lips, signaling her readiness and eagerness for him. She couldn't feign that. Bohannon always looked, always wanted to be sure she truly accepted him.

Sliding down the bed so that his shoulders were between her legs, Bohannon cupped the cheeks of her ass and dipped his tongue into heaven. He lapped at her honeyed cream as fast as she wept it. Her little clit pulsed beneath his tongue with every swipe. Just as he loved for her to do, Luna squirmed and thrust herself at him, demanding what she wanted. Her little keening cries were the sweetest music.

"Oh fuck, yes!" She cried out when he stabbed his tongue deep, followed closely by two thick fingers. "Do that! Fuck me just like that!"

She'd grown more and more bold during sex, not afraid to tell him what she wanted. After the incident, she'd found Jaz lounging in the common room, waiting for him to return. She'd been there every single day since Luna had been shot and was becoming a problem for Bohannon. Not only did he not want the woman, but he didn't want Luna uncomfortable for even a second. Luna had insisted on walking into the clubhouse on her own, not wanting to look weak in front of anyone.

Bohannon knew it had been Jaz she'd worried about. When the other woman had stood and run to Bohannon's side, Luna had calmly gone to the bar and picked up a full bottle of Jack. Jaz had thrown her arms around Bohannon and was "consoling" him for having to beat to death that "two-dollar-whore's brother."

Luna had politely tapped Jaz on the shoulder. When the other woman turned around, Luna had smiled... then calmly brought the bottle down on top of her head, breaking the bottle, spilling the whisky, and soundly knocking Jaz the fuck out. "There. That should take care of that."

Other women in the clubhouse had snickered, but helped a very groggy Jaz to the couch and cleaned up the mess. Jaz had left. The woman had been smart enough not to threaten to press charges. She was a club girl, after all. What happened in the club stayed in the club. Even leaving for new ground, Jaz wouldn't break that code. And Luna had staked her claim on Bohannon as surely as he had with her.

Luna's fingers tunneled into Bohannon's hair, clutching him tightly to her, urging him where she needed him most. When she held him in place, thrusting her hips in a wicked little shimmy, Bohannon decided she was ready.

He sat up, kneeling between her legs. Bohannon gripped her waist and flipped her over. He pulled her hips up so she was on her knees with her face on the pillow and grabbed her upper arms. With a decisive shove, he powered inside her while pulling her back onto him as the same time.

"Bohannon! Fuck! Yes! Yes!"

He set a furious, punishing pace, fucking her hard. She couldn't move, and he wanted it that way. She could only take what he needed to give her. His yells were animalistic. Hers as well. The sharp, slapping staccato of their flesh smacking against each other was furious in its pace. Soon, her ass grew red where their bodies came together.

"Say you want me," he bit out.

"I do!"

"Say you'll always want me!"

"I will! God, I will!"

"Say you'll marry me and have my children."

"You know I will! God, don't stop! Fuck me hard!"

"Going to fuck you until you can't stand it anymore! Sweet little cunt! Wet! Hot! *Ahhh!*" His orgasm exploded within him. Within her. He wanted to take her every single way he could. Every position. Wanted to give his cum a chance to quicken inside her and give him her baby. Then maybe she would never leave him.

"I'll never leave you, Bohannon," she whimpered. "Baby or not, I'll never fucking leave you ever!" Her pussy clamped down on him, wringing every last drop he had to give her. He hadn't even realized he'd spoken aloud until she'd answered him.

"I want your baby, Luna. I want our child growing inside you and still see that look of love in your eyes you always show me."

"You'll get that look, baby or not. But I want your baby growing inside me. *Our* child, Bohannon. *Ours*."

"Ours," he repeated because he couldn't help himself. Finally, he let himself roll to his side, taking Luna with him. Still he was inside her and never wanted to separate. He'd lie here until he grew hard inside her again then take her once more. He did it often. Sometimes, more than once a night. Tonight, it might be more.

"I have a confession to make," she said as she tried to catch her breath.

"Oh? Am I not gonna like it?"

She giggled. "Well, you might not like some of it, particularly the aggressive sex we just shared and both crave."

He stilled. "What? Did I hurt you?"

She instantly turned to face him, reaching her arm back to curl around his neck and bring him to her for a tender kiss. "Not in the least. Never that."

"Then what?"

"Well," she cleared her throat. "At my last checkup, the doctor had a talk with me. You'd stepped out, and he asked if I wanted him to wait on you, but you were busy getting coffee. You hadn't slept in forever and were a tad... cranky. He didn't protest and even looked at the door in relief. Apparently, I'm not the only one who thinks you're a bear if you don't get your full eight hours."

"I haven't slept much since all this happened. You can't hold that against me."

She giggled. "I don't. Anyway, he wanted to tell me he'd done some routine blood work, which, because he intended to take another CT of my head, included a pregnancy test."

"Oh, God," he whispered.

Luna grinned. "Indeed. Doc says at least six weeks, so I'm going with two months since we didn't have sex for a month after I was shot. I have an appointment with the OB in three days. I'll find out more then."

Very, very gently, Bohannon turned her over and held her close. She giggled until he let her go, frowning at her. "I don't see anything so Goddamned funny."

"You." She laughed. "Being all careful after what we just did."

"Which we won't be doing again until we know for sure everything's going to be all right. Did he mention all the drugs they had to give you for the surgery?"

"Yes. While there is a chance of adverse effects, it doesn't always happen. And we had sex the same day I was shot. It's possible the egg wasn't even fertilized until *after* all the surgery. Likely, even. It's why I put off the additional cosmetic surgery. I want to talk with the baby doctor first."

"Definitely. But I want you to know, your heath comes first. If you need a procedure, I'll want them to be as careful as possible, but I don't want to risk you. Cosmetics can be put off, but not something important."

"I don't think we'll have to worry about that. My last checkup was stellar. Hard as it is to believe, all the rest is cosmetic. Which, by the way, I'm having a hairpiece made for the back of my head. As my hair grows back, I'll trim everything up, but I'm not cutting it short. Or shaving it to my head as I'd have to right now if I wanted it even."

Finally, Bohannon found a little humor. He chuckled before he realized it. "I could give two shits about your hair. You're beautiful to me no matter what. You want a hairpiece, I'll get you thirty. You want to shave it, I'll shave mine too. We'll be bald together."

"You know, you didn't ask if the baby was yours. It is, but you didn't ask. Most men would be questioning that since we hadn't been together but a few days before everything happened. I could have been with someone else."

"Didn't have to ask. Because it doesn't fucking matter. I told you I wanted *your* baby. If it's mine, all the better. Either way, you come with any child you bear. From now on, I'll know without a doubt. Now, I'll take your word for it and be happy. *More* than happy."

Her smile lit up the world, not to mention his heart. "I love you so much, Bohannon. With all my heart, I love you."

"I love you, too. With all my heart. And I always will."

Marteeka Karland

Erotic romance author by night, emergency room tech/clerk by day, Marteeka Karland works really hard to drive everyone in her life completely and totally nuts. She has been creating stories from her warped imagination since she was in the third grade. Her love of writing blossomed throughout her teenage years until it developed into the totally unorthodox and irreverent style her English teachers tried so hard to rid her of.

Marteeka at Changeling: changelingpress.com/marteeka-karland-a-39

Changeling Press E-Books

More Sci-Fi, Fantasy, Paranormal, and BDSM adventures available in e-book format for immediate download at ChangelingPress.com -- Werewolves, Vampires, Dragons, Shapeshifters and more -- Erotic Tales from the edge of your imagination.

What are E-Books?

E-books, or electronic books, are books designed to be read in digital format -- on your desktop or laptop computer, notebook, tablet, Smart Phone, or any electronic e-book reader.

Where can I get Changeling Press E-Books?

Changeling Press e-books are available at ChangelingPress.com, Amazon, Apple Books, Barnes & Noble, and Kobo/Walmart.

ChangelingPress.com

Printed in Great Britain
by Amazon